BLABBER

Born in the UK, Morris Gleitzman emigrated to Australia with his family at the age of sixteen. His career took off as a screenwriter and a newspaper columnist, before he became a successful author. He has written a number of children's books, including *Two Weeks with the Queen*, *Misery Guts*, *Belly Flop* and *Worry Warts*. He lives in Melbourne and has two children.

Sticky Beak, the sequel to *Blabber Mouth*, is also available from Macmillan Children's Books. Both *Blabber Mouth* and *Sticky Beak* have been adapted for television, and the programme, made for Channel Four, won an International Emmy award in November 1998.

Visit Morris Gleitzman's website
at www.morrisgleitzman.com

Reviews for *Blabber Mouth*

'Very, very funny.'
Sun Herald, Australia

'Gleitzman tells his story brilliantly and with enormous humour.'
Julia Eccleshare, *The Bookseller*

Books by Morris Gleitzman

Two Weeks with the Queen

Misery Guts
Worry Warts
Puppy Fat

Blabber Mouth
Sticky Beak
Gift of the Gab

Belly Flop
Water Wings

The Other Facts of Life
Second Childhood
Bumface
Toad Rage
Adults Only

With Paul Jennings
Wicked!
Deadly!

By Mary Morris
Two Weeks with the Queen – The Play

Morris Gleitzman

Blabber Mouth

MACMILLAN
CHILDREN'S BOOKS

First published 1992 by Pan Macmillan Publishers Australia
First published in the UK 1993 by Pan Macmillan Children's Books

This edition published 1995 by Macmillan Children's Books
a division of Macmillan Publishers Limited
20 New Wharf Road, London N1 9RR
Basingstoke and Oxford
www.panmacmillan.com

Associated companies throughout the world

ISBN 0 330 39777 X

A CIP catalogue record for this book is available from
the British Library

Printed and bound in Great Britain by
Mackays of Chatham plc, Chatham, Kent

For Chris, Sophie and Ben

I'm so dumb.

I never thought I'd say that about myself, but after what I've just done I deserve it.

How could I have messed up my first day here so totally and completely?

Two hours ago, when I walked into this school for the first time, the sun was shining, the birds were singing and, apart from a knot in my guts the size of Tasmania, life was great.

Now here I am, locked in the stationery cupboard.

Just me, a pile of exam papers and what smells like one of last year's cheese and devon sandwiches.

Cheer up exam papers, cheer up ancient sanger, if you think you're unpopular, take a look at me.

I wish those teachers would stop shouting at me to unlock the door and come out. I don't want to come out. I want to sit here in the dark with my friend the sandwich.

Oh no, now Ms Dunning's trying to pick the

lock with the staff-room knife. One of the other teachers is telling her not to cut herself. The principal's telling her not to damage the staff-room knife.

I hope she doesn't cut herself because she was really good to me this morning.

I was an Orange-to-Dubbo-phone-line-in-a-heap-sized bundle of nerves when I walked into that classroom this morning with everyone staring. Even though we've been in the district over a week, and I've seen several of the kids in the main street, they still stared.

I didn't blame them. In small country towns you don't get much to stare at. Just newcomers and old men who dribble, mostly.

Ms Dunning was great. She told everyone to remember their manners or she'd kick them in the bum, and everyone laughed. Then when she saw the letters me and Dad had photocopied she said it was the best idea she'd seen since microwave pizza, and gave me permission to hand them round.

I watched anxiously while all the kids read the letter. I was pretty pleased with it, but you can never tell how an audience is going to react.

'G'day', the letter said, 'my name's Rowena Batts and, as you've probably noticed by now, I can't speak. Don't worry, but, we can still be friends cause I can write, draw, point, nod, shake my head, screw up my nose and do sign language. I used to go to a special school but the government closed it down. The reason I can't speak is I was born with some bits missing from my throat. (It's OK, I don't leak.) Apart from that, I'm completely normal and my hobbies are reading, watching TV and driving my Dad's tractor. I hope we can be friends, yours sincerely, Rowena Batts.'

That letter took me about two hours to write last night, not counting the time I spent arguing with Dad about the spelling, so I was pleased that most people read it all the way through.

Some kids smiled.

Some laughed, but in a nice way.

A few nudged each other and gave me smirky looks.

'OK,' said Ms Dunning, 'let's all say g'day to Rowena.'

'G'day,' everyone chorused, which I thought was a bit humiliating for them, but Ms Dunning meant well.

I gave them the biggest grin I could, even though Tasmania was trying to crawl up my throat.

A couple of the kids didn't say g'day, they just kept on with the smirky looks.

One of them was a boy with red lips and ginger hair and there was something about his extra-big smirk that made me think even then that I was probably going to have trouble with him.

'Right,' said Ms Dunning after she'd sat me down next to a girl with white hair who was still only halfway through my letter, 'who's on frogs today?' She looked at a chart on the wall next to a tank with some small green frogs in it.

'Darryn Peck,' she said.

The kid with the big red smirk got up and swaggered over to the tank.

'Clean it thoroughly,' warned Ms Dunning, 'or I'll feed you to them.'

We all laughed and Darryn Peck gave her a rude sign behind her back. A couple of kids laughed again and Ms Dunning was just about to turn back to Darryn when a woman came to the door and said there was a phone call for her in the office.

'Ignore the floor show,' Ms Dunning told us, giving Darryn Peck a long look, 'and read something interesting. I'll only be a sec.'

As soon as she'd gone, Darryn Peck started.

'I can speak sign language,' he said loudly, smirking right at me. Then he gave me the same finger he'd given Ms Dunning.

About half the class laughed.

I decided to ignore him.

The girl next to me was still having trouble with my letter. She had her ruler under the word 'sincerely' and was frowning at it.

I found my pen, leaned over, crossed out 'Yours sincerely' and wrote 'No bull'. She looked at it for a moment, then grinned at me.

'Rowena Batts,' said Darryn Peck. 'What sort of a name is Batts? Do you fly around at night and suck people's blood?'

Hardly anyone laughed and I didn't blame them. I've had better insults from kids with permanent brain damage.

I thought about asking him what sort of a name Peck was, and did he get a sore knees from eating with the chooks, but then I remembered nobody there would be able to understand my hand movements, and the trouble with writing insults is it takes years.

'My parents'd go for a kid like you,' said Darryn, even louder. 'They're always saying they wish I'd lose my voice.'

Nobody laughed.

Darryn could see he was losing his audience.

Why didn't I treat that as a victory and ignore him and swap addresses with the slow reader next to me?

Because I'm not just mute, I'm dumb.

'Your parents must be really pleased you're a freak,' brayed Darryn. 'Or are they freaks too and haven't noticed?'

He shouldn't have said that.

Dad can look after himself, but Mum died when I was born and if anyone says anything bad about her I get really angry.

I got really angry.

Tasmania sprouted volcanoes and the inside of my head filled up with molten lava.

I leapt across the room and snatched the frog Darryn Peck was holding and squeezed his cheeks hard so his red lips popped open and stuffed the frog into his mouth and grabbed the sticky tape from the art table and wound it round and round his head till there was none left.

The others all stared at me, mouths open, horrified. Then they quickly closed their mouths.

I stood there while the lava cooled in my head and Darryn Peck gurgled and the other kids backed away.

Then I realised what I'd done.

Lost all my friends before I'd even made them.

I ran out of the room and down the corridor past a startled Ms Dunning and just as she was calling out I saw a cupboard door with a key in it and threw myself in and locked it.

The smell in here's getting worse.

I don't think it's a cheese and devon sandwich after all, I think it's a dead frog.

I'm not opening the door.

I just want to sit here in the dark and pretend I'm at my old school with my old friends.

It's not easy because the teachers out there in the corridor are making such a racket scurrying around and muttering to each other and yelling at kids to get back in the classroom.

Ms Dunning's just been to phone Dad, and the principal's just asked if anyone's got a crowbar in their car.

It doesn't sound as though anyone has, or if they have, they don't want to go and get it.

I don't blame them. Who'd want to walk all the way to the staff car park for the least popular girl in the school?

Dad arrived just in time.

I was getting desperate because the smell was making me feel sick and Ms Dunning pleading with me through the door was making me feel guilty and the sound of an electric drill being tested was making me feel scared.

But I couldn't bring myself to open the door and face all those horrified kids.

And angry teachers.

And Mr Fowler the principal who'd skinned his knuckles trying to force the lock with a stapler.

Not by myself.

Then I heard a truck pull up outside.

I've never been so pleased to hear a vibrating tailgate. The tailgate on our truck has vibrated ever since Dad took the old engine out and put in a turbo-powered one with twin exhausts.

There were more scurrying and muttering sounds from out in the corridor and then Ms Dunning called through the door.

'Rowena, your father's here. If you come out now we'll try and keep him calm.'

I grinned to myself in the dark. She obviously didn't know my father.

I took a deep breath and opened the door.

The corridor was full of faces, all staring at me.

The principal, looking grim and holding a bandaged hand.

Ms Dunning, looking concerned.

The other teachers, looking annoyed.

Kids peeking out of classrooms, some horrified, some smirking.

Plus a couple of blokes in bushfire brigade overalls carrying a huge electric drill, and a man in a dustcoat with *Vic's Hardware* embroidered on the pocket holding a big bunch of keys, and an elderly woman in a yellow oilskin jacket with *State Emergency Service* printed on it.

All staring at me.

I don't think anybody said anything. But I wouldn't have heard them if they had because my heart was pounding in my ears like a stump excavator.

Then the door at the other end of the corridor swung open with a bang and all the heads turned.

It was Dad.

As he walked slowly down the corridor, taking in the situation, everyone stared at him even harder than they'd stared at me.

I didn't blame them. People usually stare at Dad the first time they see him. They're not being rude,

8

it's just that most people have never seen an apple farmer wearing goanna-skin boots, black jeans, a studded belt with a polished metal cow's skull buckle, a black shirt with white tassels and a black cowboy hat.

Dad came up to me, looking concerned.

'You OK, Tonto?' he asked.

He always calls me Tonto. I think it's a character from a TV show he used to watch when he was a kid. I'd be embarrassed if he said it out loud, but it's OK when he says it with his hands because nobody else can understand. Dad always talks to me with his hands. He reckons two people can have a better conversation when they're both speaking the same language.

'I'm fine, Dad,' I replied.

Everyone was staring at our hands, wondering what we were saying.

'Tough day, huh?' said Dad.

'Fairly tough,' I said.

Dad gave me a sympathetic smile, then turned and met the gaze of all the people in the corridor.

Mr Fowler, the principal, stepped forward.

'We can't have a repeat of this sort of thing, Mr Batts,' he said.

'It was just first day nerves,' said Ms Dunning. 'I'm sure it won't happen again.'

Dad cleared his throat.

My stomach sank.

When Dad clears his throat it usually means one thing.

It did today.

He moved slowly around the semicircle of people, looking each of them in the eye, and sang to them.

Their mouths fell open.

Mr Fowler stepped back.

The hardware bloke dropped his keys.

As usual, Dad sang a country and western number from his record collection. He's got this huge collection of records by people with names like Slim Dusty and Carla Tamworth—the big black plastic records you play on one of those old-fashioned record players with a needle.

This one was about lips like a graveyard and a heart like a fairground and I knew Dad was singing about me.

Part of me felt proud and grateful.

The other part of me wanted to creep back into the cupboard and shut the door.

Several of the teachers looked as though they wanted to as well.

Dad thinks country and western is the best music ever written and he assumes everyone else does too. They usually don't, mostly because he doesn't get many of the notes right.

When he'd finished, and the hardware bloke had picked up his keys, Dad put an arm round my shoulders.

'Ladies and gentlemen,' he announced, 'Rowena Batts is taking the rest of the day off. Apologies for the inconvenience, and if anyone's out of pocket, give us a hoy and I'll bung you a bag of apples.'

10

He steered me down the corridor.

Just before we went out the door, I glanced back. Nobody had moved. Everyone looked stunned, except Ms Dunning, who had a big grin on her face.

In the truck driving into town, I told Dad what had happened. He hardly took his eyes off my hands the whole time except when he had to swerve to avoid the war memorial. When I told him about the frog in Darryn Peck's mouth he laughed so much his hat fell off.

I didn't think any of it was funny.

What's funny about everyone thinking you're a psychopath who's cruel to frogs and not wanting to touch you with a bargepole?

Just thinking about it made my eyes hot and prickly.

Dad saw this and stopped laughing.

'OK, Tonto,' he said, steering with his knees, 'let's go and rot our teeth.'

We went and had chocolate milkshakes with marshmallows floating on top, and Dad did such a good imitation of Darryn Peck with the frog in his mouth that I couldn't help laughing.

Specially when the man in the milk bar thought Dad was choking on a marshmallow.

Then we played Intergalactic Ice Invaders and I was twenty-seven thousand points ahead when the milk bar man asked us to leave because Dad was making too much noise. I guess the milk bar man must have been right because as we left, a man in a brown suit glared at us from the menswear shop next door.

We went to the pub and had lemon squash and played pool. Dad slaughtered me as usual, but I didn't mind. One of the things I really like about Dad is he doesn't fake stuff just to make you feel better. So when he says good things you know he means it. Like on the pool table today when I cracked a backspin for the first time and he said how proud it made him because he hadn't done it till he was thirteen.

When we got back here the sun was going down but Dad let me drive the tractor round the orchard a few times while he stood up on the engine cover waving a branch to keep the mozzies off us.

I was feeling so good by then I didn't even mind his singing.

We came inside and made fried eggs and apple fritters, which everyone thinks sounds yukky but that's only because they don't know how to make it. You've got to leave the eggs runny.

After dinner we watched telly, then I went to bed.

Dad came in and gave me a hug.

I switched the lamp on so he could hear me.

'If you ever get really depressed about anything,' I said, 'feel free to use the school stationery cupboard, but take a peg for your nose.'

Dad grinned.

'Thanks, Tonto,' he said. 'Anyone who doesn't want to be your mate has got bubbles in the brain. Or frogs in the mouth.'

I hugged him again and thought how lucky I am to have such a great Dad.

It's true, I am.
He's a completely and totally great Dad.
Except for one little thing.
But I don't want to think about that tonight because I'm feeling too happy.

I love talking in my head.

For a start you can yak on for hours and your hands don't get tired. Plus, while you're yakking, you can use your hands for other things like making apple fritters or driving tractors or squeezing pimples.

Pretty yukky, I know, but sometimes Dad gets one on his back and can't reach it so I have to help him out.

Another good thing about conversations in your head is you can talk to whoever you like. I talk to Madonna and the federal Minister for Health and Miles from 'Murphy Brown' and all sorts of people. You can save a fortune in phone bills.

And, if you want to, you can talk to people who've died, like Mum or Erin my best friend from my last school.

I don't do that too much, but, because it gets pretty depressing.

It's depressing me now so I'm going to stop thinking about it.

The best thing about talking in your head is you can have exactly the conversation you want.

'G'day Dad,' you say.

'G'day Ro,' he answers.

'Dad,' you say, 'do you think you could back off a bit when you meet people from my new school cause I'm really worried that even if they get over the frog incident none of the them'll want to be friends with the daughter of an apple cowboy who sings at them and even if they do their parents won't let them.'

'Right-o,' he says, 'no problem.'

People pay attention when you talk to them in your head.

Not like in real life.

In real life, even if you're really careful not to hurt their feelings, and you just say something like 'Dad, could you wear a dull shirt and not sing today please', people just roll their eyes and grin and nudge you in the ribs and say 'loosen up, Tonto' and 'the world'd be a crook place without a bit of colour and movement'.

He's yelling at me now to get out of the shower because I'll be late for school and the soap'll go squishy and the water always sprays over the top of the curtain when I stand here and think.

How come he knows when a shower's going over the top, but he doesn't know when he is?

I wish I hadn't mentioned Erin because now I'm feeling squishy myself.

It's the soap that's doing it.

It's making me think of the time Erin and me put soap in the carrot soup at our school and watched everyone dribble it down their fronts, even the kids who didn't normally dribble.

This is dumb, it's over one year and two months since she died, I shouldn't be feeling like this.

I tell you what, if I ever have another best friend I'm going to make sure she wasn't born with a dicky heart and lungs.

If I ever have another best friend I'm going to make her take a medical before we start.

If I ever have one.

Dad said today'd be better than yesterday because he reckons second days at new schools are always better than first days.

He was right.

Just.

It started off worse, but.

When I walked through the gate, all the kids stared and backed away, even the ones from other classes.

Then I had to go and see the principal, Mr Fowler, in his office.

He seemed quite tense. The skin on the top of his head was pink and when he stood up to take the tube of antiseptic cream out of his shorts pocket his knees were fairly pink too, which I've read is a danger sign for blood pressure if you're not sunburnt.

'Rowena,' he began, rubbing some of the cream onto his grazed knuckles, 'Ms Dunning has told me what happened in class yesterday and Darryn Peck has been spoken to. I know this move to a normal school isn't easy for you, but that does not excuse your behaviour yesterday and I do not want a repeat of it, do you understand?'

I nodded. I wanted to tell him you shouldn't use too much cream, Dad reckons it's better to let the air get to a graze and dry it out, but I didn't in case he'd studied antiseptic creams at university or something.

'Rowena,' Mr Fowler went on, examining the graze closely, 'if there are any problems with your father, such as, for example, him drinking too much, you know you can tell me or Ms Dunning about it, don't you?'

I got my pen and pad out of my school bag and wrote Mr Fowler a short note explaining that Dad gave up drinking four years ago after he'd had one too many and accidentally spilled seventy cases of Granny Smiths in the main street of our last town.

Mr Fowler read the note twice, and I thought he was going to criticise my spelling, but he just nodded and said, 'That's all, Rowena'.

He still seemed pretty tense.

Perhaps he'd discovered his graze was going soggy.

In class everyone stared when I walked in, except Ms Dunning who smiled.

'Ah, Rowena,' she said, 'you're just in time.'

I went over to her desk and wrote a note on my pad asking if I could say something to the class.

She looked surprised, but said yes.

My hands were shaking so much I could hardly pick up the chalk, but I managed.

'Sorry about yesterday,' I wrote on the board. 'I'll pay for the frog.'

My hands were still shaking when I turned back to the class.

I was relieved to see none of the kids were backing away, and some were even smiling.

'It's OK, Rowena,' said Ms Dunning, 'the frog survived.'

The class laughed. Except Darryn Peck up the back who scowled at me.

'Thank you for that, Rowena,' said Ms Dunning.

I turned back to the board and wrote 'My friends call me Ro', and went back to my seat.

The girl next to me smiled, and suddenly I felt really good. Then I realised she was smiling at somebody over my left shoulder.

'OK, Ro,' said Ms Dunning, 'you're just in time for the sports carnival nominations.'

She explained about tomorrow being the school sports carnival and, because it's a small school, everyone having to take part.

'Right,' she said, 'who wants to be in the javelin?'

I didn't put my hand up for anything because I didn't want to seem too pushy and aggressive, not so soon after the frog. Plus you never win friends at sports carnivals. If you come first people think you're a show-off, if you come last they think you're a dork, and if you come in the middle they don't notice you.

'One hundred metres, boys,' said Ms Dunning and just about every boy in the class stuck his hand up.

When she'd finished writing down all the names, she said 'One hundred metres, girls'.

No one moved.

Then the whole class turned and looked at a girl sitting on the other side of the room.

I don't know why I hadn't noticed her before because she's got the most ringlets I've ever seen on one human head in my life. The colour's fairly ordinary, barbecue-sauce-brown, but the curls are amazing. She must keep a whole hairdressing salon in business just by herself.

Everyone watched as she looked embarrassed and raised her hand.

'Amanda Cosgrove,' smiled Ms Dunning, writing on her list. 'Who else?'

No one moved.

'Come on,' said Ms Dunning, 'Amanda can't run the race by herself.'

Amanda was looking even more embarrassed now.

Must be another new kid, I thought. I wondered what she'd done to make everyone not want to race with her, and whether it had involved jamming something in Darryn Peck's mouth.

She was looking so uncomfortable I found myself feeling sorry for her.

Which must have been why I put my hand up.

'Rowena Batts,' said Ms Dunning, writing down my name. 'Good on you, Ro. Now, who's going to follow Ro's example?'

No one moved.

'OK,' sighed Ms Dunning, 'I'll have to choose some volunteers.'

While she did, and the people she chose groaned and rolled their eyes, the girl next to me scribbled a note and passed it over.

I thought for a moment she'd got it wrong and thought I was deaf, but then I remembered that you're not meant to talk in class in normal schools.

I read the note.

'Amanda Cosgrove,' it said, 'is the 100 metres champion of the whole school.'

I smiled to myself. At least tomorrow people won't be thinking I'm a show-off. And as the rest of the people were dragged into the race, and it's really hard to sulk and run at the same time, I can probably manage not to come last.

My heart didn't sink until several minutes later.

When Ms Dunning reminded everyone that sports carnivals are family events, and she's hoping to see as many parents there as possible.

Since then I've been feeling a bit tense. Nothing serious, my knees aren't pink or anything, but I've got a bit of a knot in the guts. Not Tasmania or anything, but Lord Howe Island.

The other kids keep looking at me a bit strangely, so it must be showing.

Ms Dunning even asked if I'm feeling OK.

I reached for my notepad, then had second thoughts and just smiled and nodded.

I couldn't bring myself to tell her the truth.

That I keep having horrible visions of Dad in the middle of the oval singing to everyone, and everyone backing away.

I thought about not telling him.

I didn't tell him all the way home in the truck.

By the time we got home I felt terrible.

Here's Dad busting a gut moving us here and fixing up the house and knocking the new orchard into shape, all so I can go to a proper school and live at home, and here's me not even inviting him to the first chance he's really had to meet people in our new town.

OK, second chance if you count the conversation he had with the man in the milk bar about how if the man didn't want people to cheer and thump the wall he shouldn't have got a video game in the first place.

I mean, Dad gets lonely too.

He doesn't talk about it, but he must do.

He's left all his friends behind as well, including girlfriends.

All for me.

Even before we left he always put me first. He never invited his girlfriends to stay the night at our place when I was home on weekends because he reckoned it wasn't fair for me to get used to someone when I'd probably never see them again. That was a really thoughtful gesture because I never did see them again. His girlfriends always leave him after a couple of weeks. They're probably married to someone else and just having a fling.

All the things he's done for me, and here's me having unkind thoughts about him.

I mean, who am I to have visions about him scaring people away?

Me, who can clear a classroom in three seconds.

Two if I've got a frog in my hand.

Dad's just a slightly unusual bloke with slightly unusual clothes and a slightly unusual way with people.

I'm the psychopathic frog torturer.

Plus if he found out I hadn't told him he'd be incredibly hurt.

So I told him.

I went down to the orchard where he was spraying and jumped on the front of the tractor.

'Tomorrow's our sports carnival,' I said, 'and parents are invited. If they're not too busy. But if they are it's OK, the school understands, and us kids do too.'

The good thing about talking with your hands is people hear you even when there's a tractor roaring away and a compressor thumping and spray hissing.

The bad thing is people hear you even when, deep down, you don't want them to.

Dad stopped the tractor, tilted his hat back and his face creased with thought.

'Well, amigo,' he said, holding his thumb in the position we invented for when we want to speak with a Mexican accent, 'it's a frontier out here. Enemies all around us.'

He dropped the Mexican accent and used some of the signs we invented last week.

'Weevils,' he said, eyes darting around the orchard like a wary gunfighter. 'Weeds. Mites. Fungi. Moulds. Mildews.'

He spun round and shot a blast of spray at a clump of couch grass. The last people to run this orchard were very slack.

'On the frontier, a bloke can never rest,' he said.

I realised I was holding my breath.

Was he saying he was too busy?

'Except,' he continued, 'when it's his daughter's sports carnival. Then you couldn't keep him away even if a ten foot lump of blue mould had tied him to a railway track. What time does it start, Tonto?'

It'll be fine.

I know it will.

If I keep telling myself that, I'll get to sleep soon.

Tomorrow's just an ordinary old sports carnival and he's my dad and it's the most normal thing in the world for him to go.

It'll be fine.

It was fine.

Mostly.

Sort of.

At least Dad didn't sing.

And when he put his hand down the front of Mrs Cosgrove's dress, he was just trying to be helpful.

I'd better start at the beginning.

I got up really early and ironed Dad a shirt. One without tassels. Or pictures of cowgirls riding horses at rodeos. It had metal corners on the collar, but I hoped people would think Dad was just careful about his shirts fraying.

While he was getting dressed, Dad announced he was going to wear a special belt buckle to bring me luck in the race. I was worried for a moment, but when he came into the kitchen he was wearing one I hadn't seen before—a kangaroo in mid-hop.

I gave him a hug, partly because it was a kind thought, and partly because I was relieved he wasn't wearing the grinning skeleton riding the Harley Davidson.

In the truck on the way into town he played me one of his Carla Tamworth tapes. It was the song about the marathon runner who realises at the end of the race he's left his sweetheart's photo in the motel room so he runs all the way back to get it.

I could see Dad was trying to inspire me.

I wished he'd stop.

'Dad,' I said, 'I'm only in the hundred metres. And I'm up against an ace runner.'

Dad grinned and played the song again.

'What it's saying, Tonto,' he said, 'is that we can do all kinds of stuff even when we think we can't.'

If it was saying that, I thought, it'd be about a girl at a sports carnival who manages to persuade her dad not to upset the other spectators.

When we got to the school oval, the first event was just about to start. Kids and parents were standing around talking quietly, teachers were hurrying about with stopwatches and clipboards, and Ms Dunning was telling Darryn Peck off for throwing a javelin in the boys' toilet.

'Well, Tonto,' asked Dad, 'are we going to stand here all day like stunned fungi or are you going to introduce me to some of your classmates?'

I tried to explain that it wasn't a good time as the sack race was about to start and everyone was very tense.

'You're the only one who looks tense, Tonto,' said Dad. 'You can't win a race with your guts in a knot. Come on, lie down and we'll do some breathing exercises.'

Dad took his hat off, stretched out on the ground on his back, and started taking deep breaths through his nose.

I saw other parents glancing over with puzzled expressions, and other kids smirking.

'Dad,' I said, 'if you don't get up I'm going to drop a heavy metal ball on your head.'

Dad shrugged and got up.

As he did, Ms Dunning came over to us.

'G'day Ro,' she said. 'G'day Mr Batts.'

I explained to Dad who she was.

'G'day,' said Dad. 'Kenny Batts.' He grinned and shook her hand for about two months. 'Ro's told me what a top teacher you are.'

Ms Dunning grinned modestly and Dad turned to me and winked and asked me if Ms Dunning was married.

For the millionth time in my life I was grateful that Dad talks to me with his hands.

But I still wanted to go and bury myself in the long-jump pit.

'I can see I'm going to have to learn some sign-language,' grinned Ms Dunning. Then she excused herself and hurried away because she'd just seen Darryn Peck holding a starting pistol to another kid's head.

'Nice teacher,' said Dad. 'OK, let's mingle.'

As usual I was torn between going off and sitting in the toilets so no one could see I was with him, and sticking with him to try and keep him out of trouble.

As usual I stuck with him.

He walked over to some parents talking to their kid.

He'd already said 'G'day, nice day for it', and stuck out his hand when I realised the kid was Amanda Cosgrove, the hundred metres champion.

And Mr Cosgrove had already shaken Dad's hand and was already looking Dad up and down with a sour expression on his face when I recognised his brown suit and realised he was the bloke who'd glared at us as we were being chucked out of the milk bar.

I smiled nervously at Amanda, but she was staring at the ground.

Either that or Dad's goanna-skin boots.

'G'day,' said Dad, shaking Mrs Cosgrove's hand.

Mrs Cosgrove was looking very nervous and gripping her handbag very tightly.

'Nice suit,' said Dad, feeling Mr Cosgrove's lapel and winking at him. 'Bet it cost a few bob. Criminal, the price of clothes these days.'

'I own a menswear store,' replied Mr Cosgrove coldly.

'You'd be right then, eh?' said Dad, giving him a friendly nudge. 'Listen, you might be able to help me out. Last year at a Carla Tamworth concert one of the backup singers was wearing this unreal pink satin shirt with black fringing on the back and a black guitar on the front. I've been looking everywhere for one. You wouldn't have one in stock, would you?'

'We don't stock satin shirts,' said Mr Cosgrove, even more coldly.

Dad stared at him, amazed. 'You should,' he said, 'they're big sellers. I buy one every couple of months.'

Mr Cosgrove didn't look as though he was going to rush out and order a truckload.

Amanda nudged me gently. 'It's our race,' she said softly.

She was right.

Mr Fowler was calling through his megaphone for all the contestants in the hundred metre races. Kids were lining up in their different age groups near the starting line.

I was just about to go with Amanda to join them when I saw Dad staring at Mrs Cosgrove's chest.

Crawling across her dress was a small greyish-brown moth.

Dad took a step closer to her.

'Don't move,' he said.

Mrs Cosgrove froze with fear.

'Codling moth,' explained Dad. 'If you've got any apple or pear trees at home these mongrels'll go through 'em like guided missiles.'

'We haven't,' said Mr Cosgrove.

'I have,' said Dad, and made a grab for the moth.

Before he could get his hand to it, the moth fluttered in through the armhole of Mrs Cosgrove's dress.

Mrs Cosgrove gave a little scream.

'Hold still,' said Dad, 'I'll get it.'

He grabbed Mrs Cosgrove's shoulder and stuck his hand into the armhole.

Mrs Cosgrove gave a louder scream.

Mr Cosgrove grabbed Dad and pulled him away. 'You be careful, mister,' he snapped.

'It's OK,' said Dad, 'I've got it.'

He showed Mr Cosgrove the squashed moth between his fingers.

'You,' Mr Cosgrove said loudly, glaring at Dad, 'are a rude, unpleasant, badly-dressed hoon. Why don't you back off, go home, and leave us in peace?'

Dad stared at Mr Cosgrove, bewildered, and he looked so hurt I felt like crying.

'Amanda Cosgrove and Rowena Batts to the starting line,' boomed Mr Fowler's voice through the megaphone.

Then Dad stopped looking hurt.

He glared at Mr Cosgrove. 'Pull your head in,' he said, 'I was only trying to help.'

He turned to me. 'The bloke's a cheese-brain,' he said with his hands. 'Don't let him spoil your race. Get out there and show 'em your dust, Tonto.'

He glared at Mr Cosgrove again and walked off.

I followed Amanda to the starting line and glanced at her but she didn't look at me.

I stood there while Darryn Peck won his race and crowed about it for several minutes.

I hardly noticed.

I was seeing something else in my head.

Me doing what I should have done ages ago.

Telling Dad to back off and stop scaring people away.

Making him listen.

And him doing what I've always feared he'd do.

Looking hurt like he did with Mr Cosgrove but ten times worse because it was me, then glaring at me and walking away.

The gun went off and I leapt forward and squashed the picture in my head.

Suddenly I felt so angry I wanted to scream, but of course I couldn't so I concentrated on pounding my legs into the ground as hard as I could.

The kids on either side dropped back and suddenly the only one I could see out of the corner of my eye was Amanda Cosgrove, and then she disappeared too.

I was in front.

Then I saw Dad, up ahead by the finish line, a big grin on his face, eyes gleaming with excitement, jumping up and down and waving his arms at me.

And another picture flashed into my head.

Dad, after I'd won, sharing his excitement with the other parents.

Slapping them on the back so they spilt their drinks.

Digging them in the ribs so they dropped their sandwiches.

Sticking his hand into their armholes until they all ran for their cars and roared away as fast as they could and had serious accidents on the way home so all their kids had to go to special schools and I was the only one who didn't.

And suddenly I could hardly move my legs any more, and as I stumbled over the finish line Amanda Cosgrove was there at my side.

Sorry about that interruption, it was Dad coming in to say goodnight.

He must have noticed I've been pretty quiet since the race this afternoon because he walked into the room on his hands and he only does that when I'm depressed.

He flipped over onto his feet, or tried to, but landed on his bottom.

He didn't speak for a bit because he was using his hands to rub his buttocks and then to say some rude words. Me and Dad have got an agreement that we're allowed to swear with our hands as long as we wash them with soap afterwards.

'That's life, Tonto,' he said finally. 'Sometimes you try to pull one off and you don't quite make it. Though in my book a dead heat with the school champ's nothing to be ashamed of.'

Then he sang me a Carla Tamworth number the way I like best, with him humming the tune and doing the words with his hands. He doesn't get so many notes wrong that way.

It was the song about the axe-murderer who's a failure because his axe is blunt, but his sweetheart still loves him anyway.

Then Dad gave me a big hug.

'In my book,' he said, 'you're the champ.'

How can you be angry with a Dad like that?

'Today'll be better than yesterday,' Dad promised this morning when he dropped me at the gate, 'partly because fourth days at new schools are always better than third days, and partly because any day's better than a school sports day where the other parents are cheese-brains and the judges are bent.'

He was right.

Completely and totally.

Today is the best day of my life.

It started wonderfully and it's still wonderful.

Well actually it started strangely.

I walked through the gate and who should come up to me but Amanda Cosgrove.

'Nice turtle,' she said.

I stared at her, partly because she was the first kid to come up to me at that school, partly because I didn't have a clue what she was on about, and partly because she was speaking with her hands.

My heart was thumping and I hoped I wasn't imagining things.

Sometimes, when you're desperate for conversation, you think someone's speaking to you and they're just brushing a mozzie away.

She wasn't brushing a mozzie away.

She was frowning, and thinking.

'Good air-crash,' she said.

I still didn't have a clue what she was on about, and I told her.

She seemed to understand, because she looked embarrassed and thought some more.

I wondered if that extra bit of effort to catch up with me yesterday had starved her brain of oxygen and she hadn't fully recovered yet.

'Good race,' she said.

Her hand movements were a bit sloppy, but I understood.

I nodded and smiled.

'You're a good runner,' I said.

She rolled her eyes. 'I hate it,' she said with her mouth. 'Dad makes me do it.'

Normally I'd have been sympathetic to hear something like that, but I was too busy being excited.

Here I was having an actual conversation with another kid at school that didn't involve insults or an amphibian in the kisser.

Then something totally and completely great happened.

'Glue,' she said, with her hands.

She saw from my expression I didn't understand.

She shook her head, cross with herself, ringlets flapping.

'Twin,' she said, then waved her hand to cancel it.

'Friend,' she said.

I stared at her, desperately hoping she'd got the right word.

And that she wasn't asking if I'd seen her friend or her friend's twin or her friend's glue, she was asking if I'd be her friend.

She said it again, grinning.

I grinned back and nodded like someone on 'Sale Of The Century' who's just been asked if they'd like a mansion for $2.99.

Actually I wanted to do cartwheels across the playground, but I didn't in case she thought I was trying to tell her something about a cart.

I asked her where she'd learnt sign language, and she said on the sun.

I suggested she tell me by mouth.

She told me she'd learnt it at a summer school in Sydney, something to do with a project she's doing. Before she could fill me in on all the details, the bell rang.

It was great in class this morning because even though we sit on opposite sides of the room, we were able to carry on talking.

When Ms Dunning said something funny about Captain Cook and hamburgers, I caught Amanda's eye.

'She's nice,' I said under the desk.

Amanda smiled and nodded.

And when Ms Dunning asked Darryn Peck a question about clouds and he rabbited on for several months boasting about how his brother the cropduster pilot can do skywriting, I caught Amanda's eye again.

'He's a dingle,' I said.

She looked puzzled.

I remembered 'dingle' was a sign Dad and me had made up ourselves, so I tried something different.

She understood 'cheese-brain' and smiled and nodded.

We've just had a great lunch break sitting under a tree on the other side of the oval yakking on about all sorts of things.

She doesn't go to the hairdresser every day, her curls are natural. She told me she wishes she had straight hair like mine, and how she tried ironing it once but her dad hit the roof because he thought something was burning inside the telly.

I told her how Dad bought me some electric curlers for my birthday and tried to run them off the tractor generator to keep his legs warm in winter and they melted.

She's got a younger brother in year two who eats fluff.

I told her how I couldn't have any younger brothers because of Mum dying, and she was really sympathetic.

And when I told her about Erin I thought she was going to cry.

She's really sensitive, which can be a bit of a pain with some people, but usually isn't a problem with people who are also good runners.

She apologised for her dad losing his temper

yesterday and I apologised for Dad's antics with her mum's armhole, and we both had a laugh about how dumb parents are.

Plus we discovered we both like runny eggs.

I told her I'd make her some apple fritters.

Sometimes I had to write things down, and sometimes she had to say stuff by mouth, but the more we yakked the better she got with sign.

She even got the joke about the octopus and the combine harvester, which is only funny if you do it with your hands.

She was about to tell me more about her project, but the bell went.

It was the best lunch break I've ever had.

And now even though Ms Dunning's telling us some really interesting stuff about dinosaurs, I just can't concentrate.

I just want to think about how great it is to have a friend at last.

I wonder if Ms Dunning can see the glazed look on my face?

No problem, I'm sure she'll understand if I explain that I'm just feeling a bit mental because today's the best day of my life.

Cancel that.

This is the worst day of my life, including yesterday at the sports carnival.

No, that's not true.

The day Erin died was the worst day of my life, but at least that one started off badly with her being real crook and everything.

What I hate are days that start off well and end up down the dunny.

Like today.

This arvo everything was still fine.

Better than fine, because during art Amanda asked me if I wanted to go to her place tonight for tea.

Of course I said yes, and Ms Dunning, who I think might be a saint, or at least someone who has an incredibly well-balanced diet, let us ring Dad from the staff room to let him know.

Obviously I can't speak to Dad on the phone, except in an emergency when we've arranged I'll ring him and give three of my loudest whistles, so Amanda explained the situation to him.

'He wants to speak to you,' she said, handing me the phone.

'Tonto,' said Dad's voice, 'are you gunna be OK with that cheese-brain of an old man of hers?'

I wrote on my pad, 'Tell him I'll be fine and I promise no frogs', and gave it and the phone to Amanda.

She looked at me, puzzled, then remembered Dad was hanging on the other end.

'Ro says she'll be fine and she promises no frogs,' she told Dad, then handed me the phone.

'Right-o,' said Dad. 'I'll come and get you at eight. If cheese-brain gives you a hard time, just ring me and whistle.'

Amanda said bye from both of us and we went back to class. I felt a bit guilty not telling her what Dad had said about her dad, but at that time I still thought she was my friend and I wanted to protect her feelings.

I did have a few doubts about Amanda's dad during the rest of the afternoon.

What if he flew into a rage when I walked through the door and said something hurtful about Dad?

Or Mum?

And my head erupted again?

And he was cleaning out a goldfish bowl?

Or a hamster cage?

Or a kennel belonging to a very small dog?

I told myself to stop being silly.

I watched Ms Dunning patiently explaining to Darryn Peck that painting Doug Walsh's ears wasn't a good idea, and told myself I should be more like her.

Calm and sensible.

But I did mention my doubts to Amanda while we were walking to her house.

'Are you sure your dad won't mind me coming?' I asked.

'Course not,' she grinned. 'He'll be delighted to see I've got a community service project.'

I stared at her and felt my guts slowly going cold.

'A what?' I said.

'A community service project,' she said. 'Dad's the president of the Progress Association and they're sponsoring a youth community service drive. It's where kids find someone who's disadvantaged and help them. There's a community service night tomorrow night where we introduce our projects to the other members so they can help them too.'

My guts had turned to ice.

Amanda must have seen the expression on my face because her voice went quiet.

'I thought you could be my project,' she said.

I stared at her while my guts turned to liquid nitrogen and all the heat in my body rushed to my eyelids.

Words writhed around inside my head, stuff about how if I wanted to be a project I'd pin myself to the notice board in the classroom, and if I wanted to be a tragic case I'd go on '60 Minutes', and if I wanted everyone to point at me and snigger I'd cover myself in Vegemite and chook feathers, but I knew she wouldn't understand all the signs, and my handwriting goes to pieces when I'm angry and disappointed and upset.

'No thanks,' I said, and turned and ran.

She called my name a couple of times, but I didn't slow down.

I didn't stop running till I was halfway home and the ice in my guts was stabbing me.

I walked the rest of the way and the trees all pointed at me and whispered, 'Poor thing, she thought she'd cracked it'.

OK, I know trees can't point and whisper, but the insects did.

I decided if I ever make another friend I'll wait at least a week before I get excited.

A week should be long enough to find out if the person's a true friend, or if she just wants me for charity or to borrow money or because she needs a kidney transplant or something.

Dad was surprised to see me.

I must have looked pretty upset because he immediately switched off the tractor and the compressor and was all set to go and pay Mr Cosgrove a visit with a pair of long-handled pruning shears.

I calmed him down and told him about the community service drive.

'Tonto,' he said, his face creased the way it is when he's trying to add up the purchase dockets from the wholesaler, 'sometimes life's a big shiny red apple and sometimes it's a bucket of blue mould and disappointment.'

I nodded.

When Dad gets upset he tends to talk like a country and western song, but he means well.

'It's like the time apple scab wiped out all the Jonathans at the last place,' he said. 'I thought the potholes in my heart'd never be repaired, but they were.'

He started to sing 'Highway Of My Heart' by Carla Tamworth.

I squeezed his hand and pretended to listen, but I was thinking of Erin.

Then we went into town and had a pizza and six games of pool, which made me feel better. Dad said he'd never seen me hit the balls so hard. I didn't tell him that was because I was pretending each one was Amanda Cosgrove.

The strange thing was I couldn't sink any.

Then we came home and we've been sitting here since, listening to Dad's records.

I like doing this, because most of the songs are about unhappy people wishing their relationships had turned out better, and that's exactly how I feel about me and Amanda Cosgrove.

I wish I'd never run in that dumb race.

Because then Dad wouldn't have noticed the photo in the local paper.

'Tonto, take a squiz at this!' he yelled, bursting into the kitchen this morning.

When he gets excited he forgets and uses his voice.

I nearly dropped six eggs because the sudden noise startled me. I'd been miles away trying to work out how much batter I'd need to make enough apple fritters for a class of thirty-two kids.

OK, I know you can't buy friendship, but when the other kids think you're a psychopathic frog torturer, a plate of apple fritters might just help them see your good side.

And just because one of them's looking for a project rather than a friend, it doesn't mean they all are.

'Look,' said Dad, sticking the paper in front of my face.

There was half a page of photos of the sports

carnival, and the one Dad was pointing to was of me and Amanda crossing the finish line.

'See,' shouted Dad, 'I said the judges were bent. Look, this clearly shows you yards in front.'

I put the eggs down.

'It's the angle of the camera, Dad,' I said.

'Weevil poop,' he said. 'You're two or three centimetres in front here, easy.'

It made me feel pretty good, Dad being so indignant, but I still wish he hadn't seen the photo.

Because then he wouldn't have seen the public notice on the bottom half of the page.

'Look at this,' he said, 'your school's having a Parents and Teachers Association fund-raising bar-becue on Sunday.'

My stomach sank.

I had a vision of Dad at the P and T barbie in his most jaw-dropping shirt, the purple and yellow one, digging people in the ribs and singing at them and sword-fighting Mr Cosgrove with a T-bone steak and undoing all the good that a plate of apple fritters could ever do, even ones that had been fried in olive oil and rolled in sugar.

I raised my hands to tell him I didn't want him to go, but they wouldn't say the words. It just felt too mean, hurting him after what he'd done for me earlier this morning.

He'd come out and found me in the orchard looking for ripe apples and, when I'd told him what I wanted them for, he'd insisted on going round every tree to find the ripest.

I put my hands down and he looked up from the paper.

'Do you think Ms Dunning'll be there?' he asked, flicking his fingers so I'd think it was just a casual enquiry.

'I doubt it,' I replied. 'I think she said something about going mountain climbing in Venezuela on Sunday.'

I should have thought of something a bit more believable.

Then Dad wouldn't have given me one of his winks and said, 'Should be a good day, I think I'll wash my purple and yellow shirt'.

While he rummaged through the laundry basket, I thought frantically.

If I blew up the school, they'd have to cancel the barbie.

I told myself to stop being dumb. When you've injured people with falling masonry they very rarely become your friends. Plus it's really hard to form satisfying relationships in jail because everyone's depressed and tired from tunnelling.

Then I saw it.

An ad on the opposite page for a golf tournament. FEATURING INTERSTATE PROS it said in big letters.

I went over and pulled Dad's head out of the laundry basket.

'There's a really good golf tournament on Sunday,' I told him.

He stared at me.

46

'It's only two hours drive away and it'll be really good fun to watch.'

He continued to stare at me.

'There'll be interstate pros,' I said, trying to sound as if I knew what they were.

'I hate golf,' said Dad.

'I want to go,' I said.

'You hate golf,' said Dad.

'I know,' I said, 'but I like the coloured umbrellas.'

OK, it was a pathetic attempt, I know, but you do things like that when you're desperate.

Dad frowned, which he does when he's thinking, then his eyes lit up and he made the sign for a lightbulb going on.

'Tonto,' he said, and put his hand on his chest, 'cross my heart and hope to lose my singing voice, I promise not to start a ruckus with cheese-brain Cosgrove on Sunday arvo. OK? Now, let's get these fritters done.'

I felt pretty relieved, I can tell you.

Well, fairly relieved.

Well, I did when he said it.

We've just passed Mr Cosgrove's shop on the way to school and Dad's stuck his head out the truck and blown a big raspberry at the window display and suddenly I don't feel very relieved at all.

I made myself stop thinking about Dad as I walked into school this morning with the plate of apple fritters because I wanted to look as relaxed and friendly and approachable as possible.

All the kids rushed over, excited and curious to see what was on the plate, and I gave them a fritter each, and they gobbled them up, and they all said how yummy they were, and about six kids begged me to teach them the recipe, either at their places after school or on holiday with their families in luxury hotel suites with private kitchens at Disneyland.

That's what happened in my head.

What actually happened was that all the kids ignored me except Megan O'Donnell, who sits next to me in class.

Megan came over chewing her hair and peered at the plate. 'What's that?' she asked.

I showed her. I'd known someone would ask, so I'd written what they were on the plate.

Megan stared at the words for ages, her lips moving silently.

Then she looked up at me.

'Apple fritters,' she said.

I smiled and nodded and wished Megan spoke sign language so I could help her improve her reading. It must be really tough being a slow reader. Plus, I admit, I had a quick vision of Megan winning the Nobel Prize for Reading and being my devoted friend for ever.

'I hate apple fritters,' said Megan. 'I don't like anything with apples in. My dad works at the abattoir and he reckons apples give you cancer. He's seen it in pigs.'

I decided it probably wasn't a good idea having a best friend who would get Dad overexcited, and that Ms Dunning probably had Megan's reading under control with the extra lessons each afternoon.

I smiled at Megan and turned to look for someone else with a better appreciation of apples, and nearly bumped into someone standing right behind me.

Darryn Peck.

'Frog fritters!' he yelled. 'Batts has got frog fritters!'

He started dancing round me, his mouth bigger and redder than an elephant's bum on a cold day.

'Frog fritters! Frog fritters! Frog fritters!' he chanted.

I tried to look bored, and waited for the more sensible kids to shut him up.

They must all have been away sick because the other kids in the playground started chanting too.

'Frog fritters! Frog fritters! Frog fritters!'

The only one who didn't chant was Amanda Cosgrove.

She stood over to one side, watching with a sad expression on her face, looking as if she wanted to carry me off to an international community service conference so that the major industrialised nations could rally round and help me.

I stood there, determined not to cry.

I didn't want to give Darryn Peck the satisfaction, and I didn't want to give Amanda Cosgrove the excuse.

I couldn't understand why a teacher hadn't come over to break it up.

Then I saw why. The teachers were all over on the oval helping a man unload the marquee for the parent and teacher barbie off the back of a truck.

The chanting continued.

Darryn Peck and three of his mates clomped around pretending to be sick.

I felt volcanoes building up between my ears and suddenly I had a strong urge to remove Darryn Peck's head with a pair of long-handled pruning shears and carry it into class on the plate and feed it to the frogs.

And I didn't care what the others thought, because I didn't want them as friends.

I didn't need them.

I could survive by myself.

That's when I decided that instead of killing Darryn Peck, I'd become a nun.

I'd take a vow of silence, which would be a walkover for me, and a vow of solitude, which wouldn't be much different from how things were now, and I'd spend the rest of my life watching telly.

I was just about to walk out of the school gates to make a start, when Amanda Cosgrove did something amazing.

She walked through the chanting kids and came up to me and pulled the Gladwrap off the plate and picked up a fritter and ate it.

She looked at the other kids and chewed it with big chews so everyone could see what she was doing.

The kids stopped chanting.

Darryn Peck screwed up his face.

'Yuk,' he yelled, 'Amanda Cosgrove's eating a frog fritter!'

Amanda ignored him.

She picked up another fritter and went over to Megan O'Donnell and held it out to her and gave her a steady look.

I put the plate down to tell Amanda about Megan's problem with apples, but before I could, Megan took the fritter and started eating it.

She didn't look as though she was enjoying it.

That didn't bother Amanda.

She picked up the plate and went round to each of the kids and held it out to them.

They each took a fritter.

And by the time six or seven of them were

chewing, and nodding, and smiling, the others crowded round and emptied the plate.

'Don't eat them,' shouted Darryn Peck. 'You'll get warts on your tongue eating frog.'

Everyone ignored him, except Amanda.

'You should know, Darryn,' she said, and even his mates couldn't help laughing.

Then the bell went.

Amanda held the empty plate out to me.

'Thanks,' I said.

I decided not to be a nun after all.

We went into class without saying anything else, but halfway through the morning, when Ms Dunning asked for volunteers to go out and help put up the marquee, I glanced over at Amanda and saw she had her hand up, so I put mine up too.

Inside the marquee, while we struggled with the thick ropes, Amanda looked at me.

'I'm sorry I took you being a community service project for granted,' she said. 'I promise I'll never think of you that away again.'

Her face looked so serious in the middle of all the curls that I could see she meant it.

I couldn't answer her because I was pulling on a rope, so I gave her a smile.

She smiled back.

But even as we grinned at each other, a tiny part of me wondered if she'd be able to keep her promise.

I tried to squash the thought, but it wouldn't go away.

It didn't stop me saying yes, though, when Amanda invited me to the milk bar for a milkshake later this arvo.

We're back in class now and Ms Dunning's telling us some really interesting stuff about the early explorers.

As they sailed new oceans and explored new continents, they had this nagging problem.

They weren't sure if they could trust their navigational instruments.

I know exactly how they felt.

There's a Carla Tamworth song called 'Drawers In My Heart' about a carpenter who can make a chest of drawers with silent runners and matching knobs, but he can't make a difficult decision.

I know how he feels, because I'm having trouble making one too.

Mine's even more difficult than his.

His is pretty hard—whether to tell his girlfriend he's backed his truck over her miniature poodle—but at least he decides what to do eventually.

He makes the poodle a coffin with separate drawers for its collar and lead, and leaves it where his girlfriend will find it.

I wish I could decide what to do.

I just want everything to work out fine like it does for the carpenter, who discovers he hasn't backed over the dog after all, just a bath mat that's blown off the clothesline.

Unfortunately, life isn't that simple.

For example, you'd think going for a milkshake

with someone after school'd be pretty straight-forward, right?

No way.

Amanda was a bit quiet walking into town so after we'd got the milkshakes, to make conversation, I asked her how long her parents have had the menswear shop.

We sat on the kerb and between slurps she told me they'd had it for seventeen years, and that her dad had been president of the Progress Association for six.

Then she started to cry.

It was awful.

She looked so unhappy, sitting there with big tears plopping into her chocolate malted.

I asked her what was the matter, but she couldn't see the question so I put my arm round her.

She took a deep breath and wiped her eyes on her sleeve and said she was fine.

I was just about to say she didn't look fine when a shadow fell across us. I thought it was a cloud, but when I looked up it was Darryn Peck.

He stood there with a smirky grin on his elephant's bum mouth and a mate on each side of him.

In his hand he had a bit torn out of a newspaper.

It was a photo.

The one of me and Amanda winning the race.

'I know how you feel, Cosgrove,' he smirked. 'I'd be bawling if I couldn't beat a spazzo.'

I amazed myself.

I just sat there without throwing a single container of milkshake in his face.

I must be getting old.

Instead I reached into my bag for my notepad and wrote 'She could beat you any day, cheese-brain'. While he was reading that I wrote him another. 'We both could.'

'Oh yeah?' he said, throwing the notes down.

I nodded.

Amanda read the notes and looked a bit alarmed.

'OK,' said Darryn, 'prove it. I'll race you both to the war memorial and back and if you lose, we get to give Curly Cosgrove a milkshake shampoo.'

Amanda looked more alarmed.

I stood up.

Dad always reckons I'm a blabber mouth and he's probably right.

'A proper race,' I wrote. 'On the oval. A hundred metres. Me and you.'

Darryn read the note.

'You're on,' he said.

I wrote some more.

'The loser has to eat a frog.'

Darryn read that note twice.

Then he gave his biggest smirk ever.

'You're on,' he said.

One of his mates, who'd been reading over his shoulder, tugged his sleeve.

'That big tent's up over the running track, Darryn.'

'OK,' said Darryn, not taking his eyes off me, 'Monday lunchtime, after they take the tent down.'

He screwed the notes up and bounced them off my chest.

'Don't have any breakfast,' he smirked as he swaggered off with his mates, 'cause you'll be having a big lunch.'

Amanda unscrewed the note and read it and looked up at me as if I was a complete and total loony, which I probably am.

Before she could say anything, a voice boomed out behind us.

'Amanda,' it roared, 'get out of the gutter.'

It was Mr Cosgrove, coming out of the menswear shop.

Amanda jumped up and her shoulders seemed to kind of sag and instead of looking at him she looked down at the ground.

I didn't blame her.

His grey-green checked jacket clashed horribly with his irritable pink face.

'You're a young lady,' he snapped at her, 'not a drunken derro.'

Amanda still didn't look up.

Then Mr Cosgrove saw me, and an amazing thing happened.

In front of my eyes he changed from a bad-tempered father into a smiling president of the Progress Association.

'Hello there,' he said.

I smiled weakly and gave him a little wave.

'We're very grateful to you,' said Mr Cosgrove, 'for giving up your time this evening.'

I looked at Amanda, confused, but she was still examining the footpath between her feet.

'It would have been a rum do,' continued Mr Cosgrove, 'if the president's daughter had been the only one at the community service evening without a community service project.'

I stared at him.

I fumbled for my notepad.

But before I could start writing, Amanda spoke.

'Dad,' she said in a tiny voice, 'you've got it wrong. Ro's not my community service project.'

Mr Cosgrove stared at her.

'But three days ago you told me she was,' he boomed. 'Who is?'

'I haven't got one,' she said in an even tinier voice, still looking at the ground.

Mr Cosgrove stood there until his face almost matched his shiny dark red shoes.

'That's just about what I would have expected from you, young lady,' he said finally. 'Come on, inside.'

Amanda didn't look at me, she just followed her father into the shop.

As I watched her go, I knew I'd have to make a decision.

Do I turn my back on a friend?

Or do I allow myself to be turned into a community service project?

A helpless case.

A spazzo.

Sympathetic smiles.

Well-meaning whispers.

For the rest of my life.

I still haven't decided.

I promised myself I'd make the decision while I was walking home and I'm almost there and I still haven't.

I wish I was the carpenter in the song.

Compared to this, it'd be a breeze.

Even if I had run over the poodle.

If you've got a tough decision to make, talk it over with an apple farmer, that's my advice.

They're really good at getting straight to the guts of a matter and ignoring all the distracting waffle. I think it comes from working with nature and the Department of Agriculture.

'It's simple, Tonto,' said Dad, after I'd explained it all to him. 'If you do it, it's good for her and bad for you. If you don't do it, it's bad for her and good for you. I care more about you than her, so I don't reckon you should do it.'

I thought about Amanda at home with her angry Dad.

I thought about how her face would light up when she opened the door and saw me standing there.

Then I thought about my first day at school and how people with a temper like mine aren't cut out to be community service projects because if we crack under the sympathy who knows what we might end up stuffing into someone's mouth.

Squishy soap.

Smelly socks.

A frill-necked lizard.

'You're right, Dad,' I said.

He nodded and reached into the fridge for a sarsaparilla.

'But,' I continued, 'I'm still gunna do it.'

Dad grinned.

'Good on you, Tonto,' he said. 'I knew you would.'

Like I said, apple farmers are really simple down-to-earth people.

'I've never been to a community service night,' continued Dad. 'Hang on while I chuck a clean shirt on.'

My stomach sagged.

I hope they're also the sort of people who keep promises about behaving themselves in public.

Amanda opened the door and when she saw me standing there, she just stared.

'Can I get a lift to the community service evening with you?' I asked. 'Dad's gone on ahead.'

Yes, I know, it was a bit theatrical. Runs in the family, I guess.

Amanda's face lit up.

Mr Cosgrove's did too.

Well, sort of.

He stopped scowling and by the time we arrived at the RSL club he'd even smiled at me and told me not to be nervous because everybody there would be very sympathetic.

They were.

Amanda took me around the crowded hall and introduced me to people.

'This is Rowena Batts,' she said. 'She's vocally disadvantaged but she's coping very well.'

And everyone nodded very sympathetically.

Just before the fifth introduction I stuck a cocktail sausage up my nose to make it look as though I wasn't coping very well, but the people still nodded sympathetically.

When Amanda saw the sausage she pulled it out and glanced anxiously over at her father, and when she saw he hadn't seen it, she relaxed.

'Ro,' she giggled, 'stop it.'

'I will if you do,' I said.

She frowned and thought about this, and then, because she's basically a sensitive and intelligent and great person, she realised what I meant.

At the next introduction she just said, 'This is Ro', and I said g'day with my hands and left it to the people to work out for themselves whether I'm vocally disadvantaged or an airport runway worker.

Then I realised we'd been there ten minutes and I hadn't even checked on Dad.

I looked anxiously around the hall for a ruckus, but Dad was over by the refreshments table yakking to an elderly lady. From his arm movements and the uncomfortable expression on her face I decided he was probably describing how codling moth caterpillars do their poos inside apples, but she might just have been finding his orange shirt a bit bright.

Amanda squeezed my arm and pointed to the stage.

Mr Cosgrove was at the microphone.

'Ladies and Gentlemen,' he said, 'welcome to the Progress Association's first Community Service Night.'

I smiled to myself because his normally gruff voice had gone squeaky with nerves.

'He's vocally disadvantaged,' I said to Amanda, 'but he's coping very well.'

Amanda didn't smile.

I don't think she understood all the signs.

Then I heard what Mr Cosgrove said next and suddenly I wasn't smiling either.

'Now,' he said, 'I'm going to ask each of our Helping Hands to bring their Community Service Projectee up onto the stage, and tell us a little about them, so that we, as a community as a whole, can help them to lead fuller and more rewarding lives. First I'd like to call on Miss Amanda Cosgrove.'

I stared at Amanda in horror.

She looked at me apologetically, then took my hand and led me up onto the stage.

Everyone applauded, except for one person who whistled. But then Dad never has grasped the concept of embarrassment.

I stood on the stage and a sea of faces looked up at me.

All sympathetic.

Except for Dad who was beaming with pride.

And except for the other Projects—a bloke with one arm, a young bloke in a wheelchair, an elderly lady with a humpy back, and a kid with callipers on her legs—who all looked as terrified as I felt.

Then a strange thing happened.

As Mr Cosgrove handed the microphone to Amanda and went down into the audience, my terror disappeared.

My guts relaxed and as I looked down at all

the sympathetic faces I suddenly knew what I had to do.

I knew I had to do it even if it meant Amanda never spoke to me again.

Amanda coughed and spoke into the microphone in a tiny voice.

'Ladies and gentlemen, this is Ro and I'd like to tell you a bit about her.'

I tapped her on the arm and she looked at me, startled.

'I want to do it,' I said.

I had to say it twice, but then she understood.

'Um, Ro wants to tell you about herself,' she said, looking worried.

I made my hand movements as big and slow as I could.

'We're not projects,' I said, 'we're people.'

I looked at Amanda and I could tell she'd understood.

She gripped the microphone nervously.

I looked at her, my heart thumping, and I knew if she was a real friend she'd say it.

'Ro says,' said Amanda, and her voice started getting louder, 'that she and the others aren't projects, they're people.'

There was absolute silence in the hall.

'I'm just like all of you,' I said. 'An ordinary person with problems.'

'Ro's just like all of us,' said Amanda. 'An ordinary person with ditches.'

She looked at me, puzzled.

'Problems,' I repeated.

'Problems,' she said.

'I've got problems making word sounds,' I said, 'perhaps you've got problems making a living, or a sponge cake, or number twos.'

Amanda said it all, even the bit about number twos.

The hall was still silent.

'You can feel sympathy for me if you want,' I continued, 'and I can feel sympathy for you if I want. And I do feel sympathy for any of you who haven't got a true friend.'

I looked over at Amanda.

As she repeated what I'd said, she looked at me, eyes shining.

We stood like that, grinning at each other, for what seemed like months.

Then everyone started clapping.

Well, almost everyone.

Two people were too busy to clap.

Too busy rolling on the floor, scattering the crowd, arms and legs tangled, brown suit and orange satin, rolling over and over, fists flying.

Dad and Mr Cosgrove.

I jumped down from the stage and pushed my way through the crowd.

People were shouting and screaming, and several of the men were pulling Dad and Mr Cosgrove away from each other.

By the time I got through, Dad was sitting on the edge of the refreshments table, gasping for breath, a red trickle running down his face.

I gasped myself when I saw it.

Then I saw the coleslaw in his hair and the piece of lettuce over one ear and I realised the trickle was beetroot juice.

Dad looked up and saw me and spat out what I hoped was a piece of coleslaw and not a tooth.

'That mongrel's not only a cheese-brain,' he said, 'he's a rude bludger.'

He scowled across at Mr Cosgrove, who was leaning against the wall on the other side of the room. Various RSL officials were scraping avocado dip off his face and suit.

Amanda and Mrs Cosgrove were there too.

I caught Amanda's eye. She lifted her hands and rolled her eyes.

Parents.

Exactly.

'He called you handicapped,' said Dad. 'I told him that was bull. I told him a person being handicapped means they can't do something. I told him when it comes to yakking on you're probably the biggest blabber mouth in Australia.'

'Thanks, Dad,' I said.

'Then he called you spoiled,' Dad went on, 'so I let him have it with the avocado dip.'

Part of me wanted to hug Dad and part of me wanted to let him have it with the avocado dip.

Except it was too late, his shirt was covered in it.

I made a mental note to tell Dad avocado suited him. At least it wasn't as bright as the orange.

I took one of my socks off and dipped it in the fruit punch and wiped some of the beetroot juice off his face.

'Are you OK?' I asked.

'I'll live,' he said, 'though I feel like I've been stabbed in the guts.'

I looked anxiously for knife wounds.

'Belt buckle,' explained Dad. 'I don't think it's pierced the skin.'

He was wearing the skeleton on the Harley.

'I'd better get cleaned up,' said Dad. He looked down at himself and shook his head wearily. 'I'll never get coleslaw out of these boots,' he said, and squelched off into the Gents.

I wrung my sock out and realised that about a hundred pairs of eyes were staring at me.

As I was one of the attractions of the evening I decided I should try and get things back to normal.

I picked up the bowl of avocado dip and a basket of Jatz and offered them around.

Nobody took any.

After a while I realised why.

In the avocado dip was the impression of Mr Cosgrove's face.

It wasn't a pretty sight.

Then I looked up and saw an even less pretty sight.

The real Mr Cosgrove's face, red and furious, coming towards me.

Mrs Cosgrove and Amanda were trying to restrain him, but he kept on coming.

He stopped with his face so close to mine I could see the veins in his eyeballs and the coleslaw in his ears.

'I don't want your family anywhere near my family,' he said through gritted teeth, 'and that includes you. Stay away from my daughter.'

He turned and grabbed Amanda and headed for the door.

Amanda gave me an anguished look as he pulled her away.

There's a horrible sick feeling in the guts you get when something awful's happening and you can't do anything about it.

I got it the day Erin died.

I got it tonight, watching Amanda being dragged away.

Then I decided that tonight was different, because I could do something about it.

Or at least try to.

I ran round in front of Mr Cosgrove and stood between him and the door.

'You're not being fair,' I said.

He stopped and glared at me.

I said it again.

Then I remembered he couldn't understand hands.

I looked frantically around for a pen.

You can never find one when you need one.

I'd just decided to go and grab the bowl and write it on the floor in avocado dip, when Amanda spoke up.

'You're not being fair,' she said.

Mr Cosgrove stopped glaring at me and glared at her.

'Just because you and Dad can't be friends,' I said, 'it doesn't mean me and Amanda can't be.'

Amanda was watching my hands closely.

'Just because you and Mr Batts can't be friends,' she said to her father, 'it doesn't mean me and Ro can't be.'

Mr Cosgrove opened his mouth to say something angry to Amanda, but before he could speak, Mr Ricards from the hardware store did.

'She's got a point, Doug,' he said. 'It's like Israel and Palestine and America and Russia.'

Mr Cosgrove glared at him.

The other people standing nearby looked at each other, confused.

Me and Amanda and Mrs Cosgrove weren't sure what he was on about either.

'It's like Steve and Rob and Gail and Terry,' said Mr Ricards. 'In "Neighbours".'

The other people nodded.

It was a good point.

Mr Cosgrove obviously didn't agree, because he glared at Mr Ricards again, and then at me.

'Stay away from her,' he ordered, and stormed out.

'Mum,' said Amanda, close to tears, 'it's not fair.'

'Don't worry love,' said Mrs Cosgrove, 'he'll probably calm down in a few days,'

She turned to me.

'I don't blame you love,' she said, 'but something has to be done about that father of yours.'

She steered Amanda towards the door.

'It's tragic,' Mrs Cosgrove said to the people around her as she went. 'That poor kid's got two afflictions and I don't know which is the worst.'

Me and Amanda waved an unhappy goodbye.

I tried to cheer myself up by thinking that at least I'd be able to see her at school. Unless Mr Cosgrove moved the whole family to Darwin. Or Norway. I didn't think that was likely, not after he'd spent so many years building up the menswear shop.

After a bit Dad came out of the Gents carrying his boots.

'Come on, Tonto,' he said, 'let's go. I need to get a hose into these.'

As we headed towards the door I saw how everyone was looking at Dad.

As if they agreed with Mrs Cosgrove.

That he is an affliction.

I felt terrible for him.

We didn't say anything in the truck on the way home because it was dark.

When we got here Dad made a cup of tea, but I wasn't really in the mood, so I came to bed.

Dad's just been in to say goodnight.

He looked pretty depressed.

I thanked him again for standing up for me and offered to buy him a new pair of boots for Christmas.

He still looked pretty depressed.

I don't blame him.

How's a bloke meant to have a decent social life when everybody thinks he's an affliction?

Amanda's Mum's right about one thing.

Something will have to be done.

For his sake as well as mine.

I woke up early and was just about to roll over and go back to sleep when I remembered I had some serious thinking to do.

So I did it.

How, I thought, can I get it across to Dad that he's his own worst enemy, including weeds, mites, fungi, mould and mildews?

I could just go up to him and say, 'Dad, you're making both our lives a misery, pull your head in'.

But parents don't listen to their kids.

Not really.

They try. They nod and go 'Fair dinkum?' and 'Jeez, is that right?' but you can see in their eyes that what they're really thinking is 'Has she cleaned her teeth?' or 'I wonder if I switched off the electric curlers in the tractor?'

Who, I thought, would Dad really listen to?

That's when I decided to write him a letter.

A letter from Carla Tamworth.

It's the obvious choice.

He worships every song she's ever written.

He's always sending her fan letters and pretending he doesn't mind that she never replies.

He'll be ecstatic to finally get one.

He'll frame it.

He'll read it a hundred times a day.

I grabbed my pen and notepad.

'Dear Kenny', I wrote. 'Thanks for all the fan letters. Sorry I haven't replied earlier but one of my backup singers has been having heaps of trouble with skin rashes and I've had to take him to the doctor a lot. The doctor's just discovered that the rashes were caused by brightly-coloured satin shirts, so if you've got any, I'd get rid of them. The whole band are wearing white cotton and polyester ones with ties now and they look very nice. By the way, it's come to my attention that both you and your daughter are having problems because of your loud behaviour. In the words of my song "Tears In Your Carwash", pull your head in. Yours sincerely, Carla Tamworth. PS. Sorry I couldn't send a photo, the dog chewed them all up.'

It's a pretty good letter even though I say it myself.

I'll have to type it though, or he'll recognise my writing.

Amanda's got a typewriter.

And it's Saturday morning so her Dad'll be in the shop.

And when we've typed it I'll copy Carla's signature off one of her record covers and post it to Dad and make sure I collect the mail next week so I can smudge the postmark.

I've never forged anything before.

I feel strange.

But it's OK if there's an important reason for doing it, eh?

I hope so.

I wonder if fate'll punish me?

For a minute I thought fate was punishing me straightaway.

I went out to the kitchen with the letter under my T-shirt to tell Dad I was just popping over to Amanda's for a bit, but he wasn't there.

Then I heard his voice out on the verandah.

And someone else's voice.

Ms Dunning's.

I panicked and stuffed the letter in a cupboard behind some old bottles.

Ms Dunning's got X-ray vision when it comes to things under T-shirts. Darryn Peck had Mr Fowler's front numberplate under his on Thursday and she spotted it from the other side of the classroom.

Then I panicked for another reason.

It had suddenly occurred to me what she was doing here.

Word must have got around about the fight last night and Mr Fowler must have sent her over to tell us that the Parents and Teachers Committee had discussed the matter this morning while they were making kebabs for the barbie and I was banned from the school.

I felt sick.

I had a horrible vision of being sent away to another school and having to sneak out at night to try and see Amanda and hitchhiking in the rain and being run over by a truck.

Ms Dunning gave a loud laugh out on the verandah.

I almost rushed out and told her it wasn't funny.

Then I realised that if she was out there chuckling, she probably hadn't come with bad news.

I went out.

'G'day Ro,' said Ms Dunning with a friendly grin.

I relaxed.

'G'day Tonto,' said Dad. 'I invited Ms Dunning out to take a squiz at the orchard. She's gunna do a fruit-growing project with you kids.'

I was pleased to see Dad had remembered his manners and was speaking with his mouth.

'Your Dad's offered to come talk to the class about apple-growing,' said Ms Dunning.

Suddenly I wasn't relaxed anymore.

Dad in the classroom?

Horrible pictures filled my head.

Several of them involved Dad singing and Mr Fowler having to evacuate the school.

I pulled myself together.

Dad and Ms Dunning were heading down to the orchard. I ran after them to try and persuade them that the whole thing was a terrible idea.

As I got closer I heard Dad telling Ms Dunning about the fight last night.

Admitting the whole thing.

In detail.

I couldn't believe it.

I wondered if a person could get concussion from coleslaw.

And Ms Dunning was laughing.

She was finding it hilarious.

I wondered if chalk dust could give you brain damage.

I grabbed Dad's arm to try and shake him out of it.

He turned and gave me a look and when I saw what sort of a look it was, half irritable and half pleading, and when I heard what Ms Dunning said next, about her breaking up with her boyfriend a month ago and giving him a faceful of apricot trifle, I realised what was going on.

I can be so dumb sometimes.

Dad hadn't invited her over for educational purposes at all.

He'd invited her over for romantic purposes.

And judging by all the laughing she was doing, she wasn't feeling deeply nauseated by the idea.

I gave them both a sheepish sort of grin and walked back to the house.

Correction, floated back to the house.

Everything's falling into place.

First there'll be a whirlwind romance, with Ms Dunning captivated by Dad's kindness—he never sprays if the wind's blowing towards the old people's home—and Dad bowled over by Ms Dunning's strength of character and incredibly neat handwriting.

Then a fairy-tale wedding at apple harvest time so Dad can use one of his casual pickers as best man.

And then a happy family life for ever and ever, with Ms Dunning, who'll probably let me call her Mum by then, making sure Dad behaves himself and doesn't upset people, particularly my friends' fathers, and keeps his singing for the shower.

Keeping Dad in line'll be a walkover for a woman who can make Darryn Peck spit his bubblegum into the bin.

Suddenly life is completely and totally great.

As long as Dad doesn't stuff it up before it happens.

The first fortnight is the dodgy time, that's when his girlfriends usually leave him.

He seems to be doing OK so far, but.

When they got back to the house, Ms Dunning was still laughing, and Dad said, 'Me and Ro usually have tea at the Copper Saddle on Saturdays, care to join us?'

I struggled to keep a straight face.

The Copper Saddle is the most expensive restaurant for miles, and the closest we've ever been to it is driving through the car park blowing raspberries at the rich mongrels.

Ms Dunning said she'd love to and we arranged to pick her up at seven-thirty.

That's still two hours away and I'm exhausted.

I spent ages helping Dad choose his clothes.

I managed to talk him out of the cowgirl shirt. For a sec I thought of trying to persuade him to get a white polyester and cotton one, but then I remembered he'd have to go to Mr Cosgrove for it.

We agreed on the pale green one.

It's almost advocado.

Since then, as casually as I can, I've been trying to remind him to be on his best behaviour.

'Ms Dunning doesn't like too much chatter,' I said just now. 'She always telling us that in class.'

Dad grinned.

'Teachers are always a bit crabby in class,' he said.

Then he messed my hair.

'I know how you feel, Tonto,' he said. 'Bit of a drag, having tea with a teacher, eh? Don't fret, you'll be fine with Claire, she's a human being.'

I know I'll be fine, Dad.

What about you?

It started off fine.

When we picked Ms Dunning up she said she liked my dress and Dad's dolphin belt buckle and I'm pretty sure she meant it about both of them.

When we got here the waiter sat us at the table and Dad didn't get into an embarrassing conversation with him about shirts even though the waiter's shirt has got a big purple ruffle down the front and Dad's got a theory that shirt ruffles fluff up better if you wash them in toothpaste.

Then the menus arrived, and even though they were as big as the engine flaps on the tractor, Dad didn't make any embarrassing jokes about recycled farm equipment or taking the menus home for spare parts or any of the other embarrassing things I thought at the time he could have said.

When we ordered, he even said 'steak' instead of what he usually says, which is 'dead cow'.

I started to relax.

At least I thought I did, but when I glanced down

at my knees they were bright pink, so I was obviously still very tense.

Ms Dunning asked Dad if he was going to the parents and teachers barbie tomorrow and he said he was looking forward to it.

He asked her what would be happening there, and she went into great detail about the chicken kebabs and the raffle and the fund-raising auction and the display of skywriting by Darryn Peck's brother and the sack race and the jam stall and the wool-carding demonstration by Mr Fowler's nephew.

I was totally and completely bored, but I didn't care because I could see they were having a good time.

Then the meals arrived.

They were huge.

The pepper grinder was as big as a baseball bat, and the meals were bigger.

We started eating.

Ms Dunning asked me about my old school and I told her, but I didn't mention Erin in case my eyes went red. I didn't want Ms Dunning thinking she was marrying into an emotionally unstable family.

Dad, who was repeating to her what I was saying, was great. He didn't mention Erin either, even though he's a real fanatic about me telling the truth. He reckons if I tell lies I'll get white spots on my fingernails.

Why couldn't he have stayed considerate and quiet and normal for the whole evening?

The disaster started when Ms Dunning said she couldn't eat any more.

She'd only had about a third of her roast lamb.

Dad looked sadly at all that food going to waste and I knew we were in trouble.

At first I thought he was going to call for a doggy bag, which would have been embarrassing enough in the Copper Saddle, but he didn't.

He did something much worse.

He told Ms Dunning how he'd read in a magazine somewhere that if you stand on your head when you feel full, you open up other areas of your stomach and you can carry on eating.

Then he did it.

Stood on his head.

The waiter walked out of the kitchen and saw him there next to the table and nearly dropped a roast duck.

All the people at the other tables stared.

I wanted to hide under the tablecloth.

I waited desperately for Ms Dunning to swing into action. If Darryn Peck stood on his head in class, she'd be giving him a good talking to before you could say 'dingle'.

But she didn't give Dad even a medium talking to.

She just watched him and laughed and said that she'd read in a magazine somewhere that if you stand on your head when you're full up you choke and die.

Dad sat back down and they both laughed some more.

I can't believe it.

OK, I know that inside she's deeply embarrassed, and that after tonight she'll never want to be seen dead in the same room as Dad again.

But why doesn't she say something?

Too nice, I suppose.

That's how she can sit through all those extra reading lessons with Megan O'Donnell without strangling her.

It's tragic.

Here's Dad, pouring her some more wine and chatting away happily about why he gave up drinking, and he doesn't have a clue that he's just totally and completely stuffed up his best romantic opportunity of the decade.

Because he's his own worst enemy.

And he doesn't have a clue.

And he won't till someone tells him.

Ms Dunning won't.

So it'll have to be me.

Me and Darryn Peck's brother.

While I was creeping out of the house this morning Dad gave a shout and I thought I'd been sprung.

'Jenny,' he called out, and I froze.

I took several deep breaths to try and slow my heart down and in my head I frantically rehearsed my cover story about going for an early morning run to train for the big race with Darryn Peck.

Then I checked my nails for white spots.

Then I remembered my name isn't Jenny.

Jenny was Mum's name.

I crept along the verandah and peeked through Dad's bedroom window.

He was still asleep, tangled up in the sheet, his Elvis pyjamas scrunched up under his arms. Dad's a pretty tense sleeper and I've heard him shout in his sleep a few times. Usually it's Mum's name, though once it was 'The hat's in the fridge'.

I stood there for a few secs watching him. There was something about the way he had his arms up against his chest that made him look very lonely, and seeing him like that made me feel even more that I'm doing the right thing.

I ran into town.

Along the road the insects were waking up, and judging by the racket they were making they thought I was doing the right thing too.

'Go for it,' a couple of million screeched, and another couple of million yelled, 'He'll thank you for it later.'

One said 'You'll be sorry', but I decided to ignore that.

I went to the bank and put my card in the machine and took out my life's savings.

Then I went across to the phone box and looked up Peck in the book. There were two, but I didn't think Peck's Hair Removal sounded right, so I went to the other one.

It was quite a big fibro place with a mailbox nailed to a rusty statue of a flamingo by the gate, and two motorbikes in the front yard.

I had to ring the bell four times before the front door half opened and a bloke with a sheet wrapped round his waist and a red beard peered out.

'Are you the skywriter?' I asked him.

He stared at my note, yawning and rubbing his eyes.

'You want Andy,' he said.

He looked at me for a bit, then turned and yelled into the house.

After he'd yelled 'Andy' the third time, a bloke with red hair and a tracksuit appeared, also rubbing his eyes.

'She wants Andy,' said the sheet bloke.

The tracksuit bloke stared at me.

'Andy!' he yelled.

Another head appeared round the door.

It wasn't Andy.

It was the one I'd been dreading.

Darryn.

He stared at me in amazement, then his eyes narrowed.

'What do you want?' he demanded.

'Get lost, Dumbo,' the sheet bloke said to him.

I was glad Darryn's family knew how to handle him.

'Vanish, pest,' the tracksuit guy growled at him.

They didn't have to be so nasty about it though.

Darryn looked really hurt, and for a moment he reminded me of Dad at the sports carnival after Mr Cosgrove had called him badly dressed.

Then Darryn scowled at me and vanished.

The door opened wider and a thin bloke in a singlet and shorts stepped in front of the other two.

I guessed he was Andy because on the front of his singlet was written *Crop Dusters Don't Say It, They Spray It.*

'What is it?' he said, looking at me.

'I think she's that girl from Darryn's class,' the tracksuit guy muttered to him. 'The one he's always on about. You know, the one that can't speak cause she was shot in the throat by Malaysian pirates.'

The three of them stared at me.

Andy was looking doubtful, and I knew I had

to grab his attention before Darryn came back and started telling him more stories about me.

I decided the note I'd written explaining everything might be a bit complicated to kick off with, so I showed Andy the money instead.

He looked down at the two hundred and ninety dollars in my hand.

'Tell me more,' he said.

Where is he?

It's twenty-three minutes past four and he was meant to do it at four.

Come on Andy, please.

Perhaps he's lost the bit of paper and he's forgotten what he's supposed to write. No, that can't be it, because after he finished laughing, and agreed to do it, he wrote it on his wrist.

If he doesn't get here soon it'll be too late.

Dad'll have upset and embarrassed every parent and every teacher at this barbie and they'll form a vigilante group and we'll have to move to another town.

He's already upset the lady on the jam stall by asking if he could taste all the jams before he bought one. She laughed but I knew that inside she was ropable.

And he's embarrassed Megan O'Donnell's dad by buying twenty raffle tickets from him just because the third prize is a Carla Tamworth CD.

Mr O'Donnell shook Dad's hand and slapped him

on the back, but I could tell that inside he knows we haven't got a CD player and he thinks Dad's a loony.

And at least six people have commented how Dad's purple and yellow shirt looks as though it's made from the same material as the big purple and yellow Parents and Teachers Association banner over the marquee. They pretended they were joking, but inside I bet they were nauseous.

At least the Cosgroves aren't here.

It means I won't see Amanda today, but I'm prepared to pay that price if it means Dad and Mr Cosgrove won't be stabbing each other with chicken kebabs.

Four twenty-four.

Come on, Andy.

Perhaps he's got mechanical trouble. No, that can't be it, everyone knows crop-dusters keep their planes in A-1 mechanical condition. Farmers won't hire you if you keep crashing into their sheds.

I've got a knot in my guts the size of Antarctica.

Relax, guts, it'll be fine.

That's the great thing about talking in your head. It takes your mind off stress and you don't get ulcers. If I wasn't having this conversation now I'd be a nervous wreck.

Oh no.

I can't believe what Dad's just done.

He's donated a song to the fund-raising auction.

He actually expects people to bid money for him to sing them a song.

This is so embarrassing.

I'd go and hide in the marquee if I didn't have to keep an eye out for Andy in case he's having trouble with his navigational equipment and I have to set fire to some chicken kebabs to guide him in.

Dad'll be so hurt when nobody bids.

I can picture his face now.

Good grief, someone's just bid.

Two dollars, that's an insult.

Haven't these people got any feelings?

And now four dollars from Doug Walsh's parents.

What are you trying to do, destroy my father's self-respect?

Dad's grinning, but inside he must be feeling awful.

Stack me, Ms Dunning's just bid ten dollars.

Why's everyone laughing? At least she's doing her best to make him feel better.

Oh.

The ten dollars is for him not to sing.

Mr Fowler has banged his auctioneer's hammer and declared her the successful bidder.

Everyone's laughing and clapping, including Dad, but inside he must be bleeding.

Four twenty-seven.

Andy, this is getting desperate.

I know skywriting is just a hobby for you, but it's a matter of life and death down here.

Now Ms Dunning's trying to persuade Dad to go in the sack race.

That woman is incredible.

Even though he's taken the sack off his feet and put it on his head and she must be burning up inside with embarrassment, she's still pretending she's enjoying herself so she doesn't hurt his feelings.

Definitely a saint.

Four twenty-eight.

Where is he?

If Andy Peck has flown to Western Australia with my two hundred and ninety dollars I'll track him down even if it takes me the rest of my life because it took me hundreds of hours helping Dad in the orchard to earn that money.

There's Amanda.

She must have just arrived.

Oh well, at least now I've got someone to moan to about the Peck family.

Oh no, if she's here, that means . . .

Mr Cosgrove.

There he is.

He's seen Dad.

Don't do it, Dad, don't take the sack off your head.

He's taken it off.

He's seen Mr Cosgrove.

They're staring at each other.

Oh no.

Wait a sec, what's that noise?

Is it . . ?

Yes.

It's a plane.

Andy Peck turned out to be a really good skywriter for an amateur.

Though as I'd paid him two hundred and ninety dollars I suppose that made him a professional.

Anyway, he did a great job and I'm really happy. Fairly happy.

I think.

His letters were big and clear, huge swoops of white smoke against the blue sky.

As the plane started buzzing overhead, Mr Fowler stopped the charity auction. 'We'll take a breather,' he said, 'and enjoy the spectacle.'

Most people were already looking up.

'What's he writing?' asked a woman near me.

The Parents and Teachers Committee asked him to write the school motto,' said a man.

'I didn't think the school motto began with "Pull",' said the woman.

'Nor did I,' said the man, frowning as he looked up at the huge PULL hanging in the sky.

'It doesn't,' Amanda said in my ear. 'The school motto's "Forward Not Back".'

'He's not doing the school motto,' I said. 'He's helping me save my dad's social life.'

Amanda stared at me.

I looked over at Dad.

He wasn't even looking up. He was walking towards Mr Cosgrove.

That's when I got mad.

I wanted to yell at him.

'Listen, you cheese-brain,' I wanted to roar, 'I'm trying to tell you something.'

But you can't yell with your hands across a crowded school oval.

I was nearly exploding.

It was an emergency.

I put my fingers in my mouth and gave three of my loudest whistles.

Dad stopped and looked around and saw me.

I glared at him and pointed up.

He looked up.

Andy had almost finished the YOUR.

Dad stared.

So did Mr Cosgrove.

So did Amanda.

So did everyone.

Nobody spoke until Andy had finished HEAD, then a buzz of voices started.

Amanda gripped my arm. 'You didn't?' she gasped.

I was still glaring at Dad.

He was still peering up, puzzled.

Andy finished the IN.

' "Pull Your Head In," ' someone read. 'That's not the school motto.'

'It is now,' someone else said, 'so pull your head in.'

Everyone laughed.

I wanted to scream at them. Couldn't they see this was serious?

Andy finished the DAD.

Everyone went quiet again.

Dad was staring up, not moving a muscle.

Then he turned and looked at me.

I looked back at him as calmly as I could, even though my heart was thumping like a ten-million-watt compressor.

It was so loud I could only just hear the plane flying off into the distance.

Then everyone started talking in puzzled tones and Amanda grabbed my arm again.

'How did you do that?' she said.

The people around us stared.

'I wish I could get my Dad to pay attention like that,' said Amanda wistfully. 'Gee, you're clever.'

I looked at her wide-eyed face and hoped she was right.

Because when I looked back over at Dad, he'd gone.

I knew that would probably happen. I knew he'd need a few moments to think about it. Before we talk.

The other parents were whispering and pointing

at me and frowning, but I could tell that inside they knew it had to be done.

After a few moments I went looking for Dad.

He wasn't in the marquee.

He wasn't in any of the classrooms.

He wasn't in the Gents.

I went back to the oval thinking perhaps he'd decided to buy a book called *How To Win Friends And Influence People* which had been the next item in the auction, but when I got there the auction was over and people were starting to leave.

Amanda came running up.

'I just saw him driving out of the car park,' she said breathlessly.

I knew that might happen. I knew he might need a bit longer to think about it. Before we talk.

Amanda was looking at me in a very concerned way, so I explained to her that everything was under control.

Ms Dunning saw me and started to come over, but then Darryn Peck, who'd got overexcited at his big brother being the centre of attention, managed to set fire to one of the marquee flaps and Ms Dunning had to attend to that.

Mr and Mrs Cosgrove came over.

Mr Cosgrove was beaming.

'Well, young lady,' he said, 'for someone who can't speak, you certainly put that loud-mouthed father of yours in his place.'

Amanda squeezed my hand, which helped me not to do anything ugly.

They've just given me a lift home.

I made Mr Cosgrove drop me at the bottom of the orchard road because I don't think Dad'll want to see him at the moment.

I'm not even sure he'll want to see me.

Searching the orchard was a waste of time because after I'd searched the house and the shed I realised the truck'd gone so it stands to reason he has too but I searched the orchard anyway because a tiny part of me was hoping he was playing the game we used to play when I was a little kid where he'd hide in our old orchard and I'd have to try and find him and as I got closer and closer he'd make little raspberry noises with his mouth to give me a clue and when I found him he'd let me walk back to the house in his boots even though they came over my knees and I did a pee in one of them once.

He wasn't.

He's gone.

If I say it in my head enough times I'll get used to it and stop feeling so numb and then I can think what to do.

He's gone.

He's gone.

He's gone.

I'm still numb.

I can't even stand up.

I've been sitting here since I came back from the orchard and saw the letters on the kitchen table.

One was my letter to him from Carla Tamworth.

The other was in his writing on a piece of Rice Bubbles packet.

'Dear Ro,' it said, 'I feel pretty crook about all this and I don't want to think about it right now so I'm taking a hike. Go and stay with Amanda. Dad.'

He never calls me Ro.

On the table under the letters was eighty dollars.

Then I saw the cupboard where I'd stuffed the Carla Tamworth letter.

The door was open and the old bottle of rum that Dad hadn't chucked away in case a visitor wanted a drink was lying on the floor.

Empty.

That's when I knew I'd lost him.

Amanda and her family were pretty surprised when I arrived on the tractor.

They came out onto their front verandah and stared.

I explained what had happened, and how I'd needed the tractor because I'd brought all my clothes with me and I'd never have got the suitcase to their place by hand.

Mr and Mrs Cosgrove made me explain it all again.

Isn't it amazing how you can still do complicated explanations even when you're completely and totally numb inside your head?

Amanda was great.

She rushed over and dragged the suitcase off the tractor and said I could stay with them for the rest of my life if I wanted to.

Mr and Mrs Cosgrove were good too.

After I'd parked the tractor in their driveway next to their car and the colour had come back into their cheeks, they took me into the house and gave me a glass of pineapple juice and some chocolate biscuits and a toasted ham and cheese sandwich.

Even Amanda's little brother Wayne was fairly good.

When he'd finished telling everyone I couldn't have his room and I wasn't allowed to use his cricket gear or his bug-catcher or his video games, he disappeared and came back with a toothbrush which he said I could share with him as he only used it to clean the points on his train set about once a week.

I thanked him and explained I'd brought my own.

Amanda and me went and made up the camp bed in her room.

Then we sat on it and Amanda asked how I felt. 'Numb,' I said.

Even saying that one word wasn't easy because suddenly my hands were shaking so much.

She looked at me, concerned and puzzled.

'I don't understand,' she said. 'You feel like a dentist?'

I was just about to tell her again when suddenly I didn't feel numb any more, I felt completely and totally sick and I had to run to the toilet.

I wasn't sick but I had to lean against the wall while I shivered and cold sweat dripped off me.

Amanda's anxious voice came through the door. 'Are you OK?' she asked.

I opened the door and told her I'd be fine and that I'd see her back in her room.

I didn't want her skinning her knuckles trying to open the door with a knife.

After a bit I felt less shaky, so I came out.

On my way back I stopped in the hallway because I could hear Mr and Mrs Cosgrove talking about me in the living room.

'Sergeant Vinelli said there's not much they can do tonight,' said Mr Cosgrove. 'They'll put out a search call for him in the morning. Oh, and Child Welfare will have to be informed.'

'I'll see Mr Fowler at school tomorrow,' said Mrs Cosgrove. 'He's probably the best person to handle it. Poor kid. We should get the Community Service Committee to start a fund to help tragic cases like hers.'

'I hope they catch that hoon,' said Mr Cosgrove, 'and throw him in jail.'

I almost went in there and asked him how he'd feel if he'd just been humiliated in front of half the town.

But I didn't because, let's face it, you probably can't change people.

Mr Cosgrove'll probably always hate Dad and Dad'll probably always love eye-damaging shirts and there's probably nothing me or the Prime Minister or anyone can do about it.

Anyway, I didn't have the energy for another run-in with Mr Cosgrove because what with reading Dad's letter, and having the shakes in the bathroom, and standing there in the hallway realising I was back to being a project, I was feeling pretty depressed.

I went back to Amanda's room and went to bed.

'Ro,' said Amanda, 'I'm sorry about your dad, but I'm really glad you're here.'

'Thanks,' I said.

Mr and Mrs Cosgrove came in and said goodnight, and Mrs Cosgrove squeezed my hand and said she was sure everything would turn out fine.

I think it was them kissing Amanda that did it.

Suddenly I missed everyone so much.

Mum.

Erin.

Dad.

I managed to hang on till Mr and Mrs Cosgrove had switched the light out and closed the door, then I felt something rushing up from deep in my guts and the tears just poured out of me.

I didn't want them to, not in someone else's house, but I couldn't help it.

I pushed my face into the pillow and sobbed so hard I thought I'd never stop.

Then I felt someone get into the bed behind me.

It was Amanda.

She put her arms round me and stroked my hair while I cried and suddenly I didn't feel like a project at all, just a friend.

It's amazing how much better you feel after a cry and a sleep.

I reckon if people had more cries and sleeps, they woudn't need half the aspirin and ulcer medicine and rum in the world.

I don't feel numb this morning, or sick.

Just sad.

But life must go on.

That's what my teacher at my old school said after Erin died. The human organism, she said, can survive any amount of sadness if it keeps busy. She was a doctor, so she knew.

I'm keeping busy now.

I'm having this conversation in my head.

Plus I'm making apple fritters for Mr and Mrs Cosgrove and Amanda and Wayne's breakfasts.

Plus I'm putting a lot of effort into not making too much noise because it's only five-thirty and I don't want them to wake up till the fritters are done.

Plus I'm thinking.

I'm thinking how even though I feel very, very sad, I feel kind of relieved too.

All my life I've had this worry, deep down, that Dad would leave.

Now I don't have to worry about it any more, because he has.

I don't blame him, not really.

He's got his life too.

Who knows, he might finally meet a woman who doesn't embarrass easily and they might have a baby and he might finally get to have a daughter who can speak.

I wish I hadn't thought that, because now I'm crying again.

This morning would have been a disaster without Amanda.

First, while I was sitting in the kitchen making the drying-up cloth all soggy with tears, she smelt the smoke from the fritters and ran in and pulled them off the stove before the kitchen burnt down.

Then, when Mr Cosgrove came rushing out of his bedroom with a fire extinguisher, she explained to him that I always make fritters when I'm depressed, plus they were for his breakfast.

He shouted quite a bit, but she stood up to him.

I was proud of her.

Then, after Mrs Cosgrove had driven us to school and had gone off to see Mr Fowler, Amanda took my arm and we walked in through the gate together.

It's amazing how quickly word gets around in a small country town.

Every kid in that playground just stood and stared.

'What's the matter with you lot?' said Amanda. 'Haven't you ever seen an abandoned kid before?'

It wasn't the best line I'd ever heard, but it was better than I could have done at the time, and I was really grateful.

Everyone carried on staring.

Except Darryn Peck.

He swaggered over and I saw he was carrying a jar with a frog in it.

The biggest frog I'd ever seen.

Then I remembered.

The race.

'S'pose you'll want to chicken out now,' Darryn said to me with a smirk.

Amanda took a step towards him.

'She's not chickening out,' she said, 'she's just not feeling well. I'll race you.'

'Loser eats this,' said Darryn, holding up the frog.

'I know,' said Amanda.

I felt like hugging her, but I didn't because emotionally deprived kids like Darryn Peck don't understand real friendship and they use it to get cheap laughs.

'Thanks,' I said to her, 'but I want to do it.'

I think she understood what my hands were saying.

Anyway, she understood what my face was saying.

I turned to Darryn and poked myself in the chest, and then poked him in the chest.

He understood what I was saying.

'Lunch time,' he said.

I nodded.

The frog gurgled.

All morning in class Ms Dunning behaved very strangely.

She hardly looked at me, and didn't ask me a single question.

To show her I needed to be kept busy, one time when she asked Megan O'Donnell a question I just walked out the front and wrote the answer on the board.

It didn't make any difference. I still spent the rest of the morning with my hand in the air, being ignored.

I couldn't understand it.

I looked at Amanda and I saw she couldn't understand it either.

Then things became clearer.

The lunch bell went, and Ms Dunning said, 'Ro, could I see you in the staff room please?'

The staff room was deserted because the other teachers were out on the oval taking down the marquee.

Usually when a teacher and a kid have a conversation in the staff room, the teacher stands still and the kid does a lot of nervous shuffling about.

Today with me and Ms Dunning it was the opposite.

I stood there while she did a lot of nervous shuffling about.

'Ro,' she said, 'before your dad disappeared, did he say anything about me?'

I shook my head.

Ms Dunning shuffled some more.

She looked pretty worried.

I wrote her a note.

'What's the matter?' I asked.

She read it and took a deep breath, but didn't say anything.

'It's OK,' I said, 'I won't blab to anyone else.'

She read that and gave a worried little smile.

'Ro,' she said after what seemed like a couple of months, 'your dad wants me to be his girlfriend, but I don't.'

I nodded. I knew that.

'And,' continued Ms Dunning, 'I told him that yesterday, just before your message in the sky, just before he disappeared.'

I didn't know that.

'And,' Ms Dunning went on, 'I'm worried that's why he's gone missing.'

I wrote her a long note telling her not to be silly, that my message was the reason he'd gone. Writing it made me feel incredibly sad. To cheer us both up, I asked her to be the line judge for my race with Darryn Peck.

She smiled and said yes.

Most of the school was out on the oval, lining both sides of the running track.

As Ms Dunning took her position, she saw the frog in the jar on the other side of the finish line.

'What's that?' she asked.

The whole school held its breath.

I did too.

If the race was banned now, Darryn'd be crowing for months about how he'd have won.

'It's what they're racing for,' said Amanda.

That girl's a future Prime Minister.

Ms Dunning gave a tired smile and said, 'I can think of more attractive prizes'.

As I walked to the start line, Amanda ran up and squeezed my arm. 'Don't slow down at the end like you did with me,' she said. 'Keep going.'

I didn't know she'd noticed.

But I was too tense to say anything.

I nodded and crouched down next to Darryn on the start line.

'They're good with cheese sauce, frogs,' he smirked, but before I could answer, Ms Dunning blew her whistle and I flung myself forward.

It wasn't a good start and I was off-balance for the first few steps.

Out of the corner of my eye I could see Darryn moving ahead.

I pounded my legs harder, but I couldn't get past him.

Sweat was running into my eyes.

We got closer and closer to the finish line.

Then I saw it. Next to Ms Dunning. A blur of bright purple and yellow. And I knew it was Dad.

I could see him waving his arms in the air, just like he did in the race with Amanda.

Suddenly my legs felt light as whips and I knew I was going to win.

I didn't care if Dad got so excited he kissed all

the teachers and made them all drop their lunches and stuck his hand into all their armholes.

That was his problem.

I was level with Darryn.

The finish line was rushing towards me.

I stretched my arms out and hurled myself at the excited purple and yellow blur and crossed the line with Darryn's feet thundering at my heels.

There was shouting and cheering and Amanda threw her arms round me and squeezed me so hard I couldn't suck air.

I barely noticed.

All I was really aware of was the purple and yellow blur, which now I was up close wasn't a blur at all.

It was the Parents and Teachers Association banner, rolled up in the arms of a teacher, a loose end flapping in the breeze.

Dazed, I turned away.

I felt sick, but that might have just been the run.

Keep busy, I thought, keep busy.

Darryn was sprawled on the ground, looking as sick as I felt.

His eyes flicked up at me, and then at the frog, and then at the ground again.

Just for a sec, while he was looking at me, he had the same expression he had yesterday after his brothers had been mean to him.

Suddenly I wanted to tell him to go home and tell his brothers to pull their heads in.

111

It wasn't the time to do that, so I found my bag and pulled out my lunch box and pulled out the apple fritter I'd been planning to pick the burnt bits off and have for lunch.

I held it out to Darryn.

He looked at it, then at me, puzzled.

I found my pad and pen but before I could write anything, Amanda spoke up.

'Frog fritter,' she said to Darryn.

What a team.

Darryn took the fritter, and just for a fleeting second I thought he looked grateful.

Hard to tell, on a face that spends so much of its time smirking.

I picked up the frog in the bottle and turned to ask Ms Dunning if she thought it would eat the other frogs in our classroom.

While I was writing there was a shout.

Mr Fowler, pink and agitated, was hurrying towards Ms Dunning.

'That blessed girl's locked herself in the stationery cupboard again,' he said.

Then he stopped and stared at me.

'Well someone has,' he said.

Everyone stood there for a bit.

Then I remembered and my heart tried to get out through my mouth.

Even though my lungs were still sore I made it into the school in about three seconds.

In the staff-room corridor I stopped in front of the stationery cupboard door and took the biggest breath I could and started to whistle 'Heart Like A Fairground' by Carla Tamworth.

I can whistle loud, but I'm a bit crook on tunes.

Mr Fowler and Ms Dunning and a crowd of kids arrived and they all stared at me as if I was loony.

I didn't care.

There was a rattle at the keyhole and the cupboard door swung open and there was Dad.

'About time,' he said. 'I forgot the peg and the pong in here'd strip paint.'

It was my turn to stare.

He was wearing a grey suit and a white shirt and a brown bow tie.

The suit was too short in the arms and the legs.

The shirt was so big that the bow tie was sticking up over his chin.

I didn't know whether to collapse into giggles like Ms Dunning was doing or forget that half the class were there and burst into tears.

'Dad,' I said, 'you look ridiculous.'

He gave me a nervous grin.

'That's what happens when you buy your clothes from a cheese-brain,' he said. 'Bludger doesn't have anything in your size.'

We gave each other a huge hug, though it wasn't easy for him because he couldn't move his arms that much.

Even though I was so happy I could hardly think, I made a mental note that brightly-coloured satin shirts are much more generously cut than suits, and therefore much better for cuddles.

Then, after he went and had a chat to Mr Fowler and Sergeant Vinelli and persuaded them that any man in a suit must be a responsible father, he took me and Amanda back to our place and we built a big bonfire and had sausages and marshmallows for tea.

After Dad got changed I was tempted to chuck the suit onto the fire.

I didn't.

I decided it might be useful to have it around, in case Dad gets out of hand again.

I might be totally and completely happy, but I'm not dumb.

Morris Gleitzman
Sticky Beak

*There are times when it's a real pain not being able to speak.
You want to scream with frustration, except of course you
can't. So you make do with what you've got.*

*I put my face close to the cocky's and gave it a look. 'Don't be
scared, you poor little thing,' the look said. 'I want to help
you.'*

'Rack off,' said the cocky.

Rowena Batts has enough problems in her life without
adopting a crazy cockatoo. For a start, she's just splattered
two hundred grown-ups with jelly and custard.

But a crazy cockatoo, Ro discovers, can turn out to be just
the friend she needs . . .

'Side-splitting humour' JUNIOR BOOKSHELF

The hilarious and heart-warming sequel to *Blabber Mouth*.

Morris Gleitzman
Misery Guts

*Keith's heart was pounding. Calm down, he thought. You're
not robbing a bank. You're not kidnapping anybody. You're
just painting a fish and chip shop orange.*

Keith is trying to cheer up his parents. But a pair of misery
guts need more than a pot of Tropical Mango Hi-Gloss to
make them happy. What they really need, Keith decides, is to
live in Paradise.

Trouble is, Paradise is halfway round the world.

Even Keith Shipley is stumped by that one. Almost.

'Totally compelling' CHILDREN'S BOOKS OF THE YEAR

'Great Fun' BOOKS FOR KEEPS

Morris Gleitzman
Worry Warts

Dear Mum and Dad,

This is just to let you know that I took the torch, the hammer, the gardening trowel, the plastic strainer, the chocolate biscuits and the stuff that's missing from the bathroom. So it's OK, you haven't been burgled. Please don't worry, things are looking even better than I thought, opal-wise.

Love, Keith

Going down a mine and digging up a fortune in precious opals is Keith's solution to his parents' problems. Stacks of money will make everything OK in their tropical paradise, and save them from being permanent worry warts.

Won't it?

Another brilliant Keith Shipley plan – if it works . . .

Morris Gleitzman
Puppy Fat

*'What section do you want to advertise in? Toys? Sporting
Equipment? Computers and Video Games?' The woman in the
newspaper office took off her glasses and polished them on
her cardigan. 'What are you advertising?'*

'My parents,' said Keith.

Keith's worried. Can two single parents with saggy tummies,
wobbly bottoms and dodgy legs ever find happiness? Not a
chance, decides Keith, unless he can get them into shape.
Just as well Tracy the mountaineer and Aunty Bev the
beautician are arriving from Australia . . .

The brilliantly funny sequel to *Misery Guts* and *Worry Warts*.

A selected list of titles available from Macmillan Children's Books

The prices shown below are correct at the time of going to press. However, Macmillan Publishers reserve the right to show new retail prices on covers which may differ from those previously advertised.

MORRIS GLEITZMAN

Title	ISBN	Price
Blabber Mouth	0 330 39777 X	£4.99
Sticky Beak	0 330 39778 8	£4.99
Misery Guts	0 330 32440 3	£3.99
Worry Warts	0 330 32845 X	£3.99
Puppy Fat	0 330 34211 8	£3.99
Belly Flop	0 330 39824 5	£4.99
Water Wings	0 330 39825 3	£4.99

All Pan Macmillan titles can be ordered from our website, www.panmacmillan.com, or from your local bookshop and are also available by post from:

**Bookpost
PO Box 29, Douglas, Isle of Man IM99 1BQ**

Credit cards accepted. For details:
Telephone: 01624 836000
Fax: 01624 670923
E-mail: bookshop@enterprise.net
www.bookpost.co.uk

Free postage and packing in the UK.